## *Meet the DForce i*

**MARK STONE.** He<...> former Green Bere<...> voted his life to finding America's forgotten soldiers in Vietnam and freeing them from their hell on Earth. His rescue tactics are unique—and quite lethal.

**HOG WILEY.** He's a good ole boy from East Texas—and one of the deadliest mercenaries money can buy. This burly bulk of southern-fried fury loves fighting almost as much as he loves whiskey and women. And that's why he's perfect for Stone's team.

**TERRANCE LOUGHLIN.** He's a steely British commando with a refined taste for culture—and total destruction. Explosives are his specialty, but this tough Englishman can fill a walking target with bullets like a master assassin.

*These guys are the very best. And the U.S. government knows it. In fact, they may be America's only hope in the most desperate international situations.*

*No job is too tough for...*

## *Stone: M.I.A. Hunter*

Don't Miss the Others in This Action-Packed Series!

# STONE
# M.I.A. HUNTER
## CROSSFIRE KILL
### JACK BUCHANAN

JOVE BOOKS, NEW YORK

STONE: M.I.A. HUNTER
CROSSFIRE KILL

A Jove Book/published by arrangement with
the author

**PRINTING HISTORY**
Jove edition/January 1989

ISBN: 0-515-09869-8

10  9  8  7  6  5  4  3  2  1

*"Go with us as we seek to defend the defense-less and to free the enslaved."*

—from the "Special Forces Prayer"

# Chapter One

*Paris, in the spring . . .*

Webster Rankin put out his cigarette and opened the garage door as the black Renault came into the shadowy alley. Overhead, high in the afternoon sky, a plane droned past, and a few birds quarreled in the trees nearby.

The Renault bumped along the rutted alleyway, turning into the garage. Danzig switched off the engine and nodded to him. Rankin pulled the door closed from the inside. He dropped the length of wood into the two slots, locking it, then switched on the overhead light.

Danzig got out of the car carrying a long, plastic-wrapped bundle. "It'll soon be summer, " he said. A short, potato-faced man with a black mustache, Danzig looked to be about forty-five. He stretched his arms, pulled his dark overcoat straight and handed the bundle to Rankin. His English was excellent. "Are you nervous?"

"I feel fine," Rankin said gruffly. "Did you bring the money?" He was taller, dressed in nondescript clothes like a workman. He wore a shapeless cap and had a two-day beard. He had walked the last mile to the garage, shoulders stooped and hands in pockets with a cigarette in the corner of his mouth. But no one, he thought, had given him a second glance. He would leave in the car with Danzig, and the neighborhood would never see him again.

Danzig patted his pocket. "Of course. And the ticket as well."

1

"Good." Rankin stepped to the small door at the rear of the garage. Stairs led through another door into the house. He went up silently, breathing dust. The house was dark and smelled of old, rotted wood and other, unidentifiable odors. He had been here once before, a month ago, and nothing was changed; Danzig had assured him.

Rankin felt good about this job. It meant he would be going home to the States in the morning. He hadn't been home in twelve years. He was a morose, hollow-cheeked man with a shock of straight brown hair that flowed past his ears; he had been letting it grow for the last month, since Danzig had approached him with the proposition. As soon as the job was over he'd get it cut short. A man couldn't be too careful.

At the top of the stairs was a dark hallway, lit only by a dirt-clotted skylight. No one lived in the building. It was slated to be torn down; the front was all boarded up and there was no stairway to the street. They went along the gloomy hall, into the end room. It was unexpectedly large and had no furniture but an old table and one chair. There was a brown-stained sink against one wall and the two windows were still hung with torn, greasy curtains. The windows overlooked the street, and Rankin stood, looking down at the spot where his victim would die.

Danzig closed the door behind them. "Are you all right?"

"Of course." Rankin looked at the other in surprise. But this kind of thing must be new to Danzig. He watched the man light a cigarette, saw his fingers tremble. Danzig was the one who was nervous. He turned back to the window.

It was a neighborhood of small shops and multiple dwellings, on the edge of a more respectable district. People came and went at all hours.

"Let's see the money," Rankin said.

Danzig made a face. He took a thick wallet from his coat and pulled out a packet. "Ten thousand dollars, American. Count it." He dropped it on the table between them.

Rankin picked up the money and thumbed it, sure it was correct. Danzig wouldn't have the guts to cheat him. He put the money away and stepped to the window again.

Across the street was a row of shops: Epicerie, Ready to Wear, Boulangerie, Chez Surin. In between two of them was a recessed doorway that led up to the second-floor apartments.

Danzig pointed. "Our man will get out of his car opposite that door. There are three steps from the car to the door. There is a girl. . . ."

Rankin looked at him. "Nothing has changed?"

"You asked that before. Nothing. It is the way we planned."

"You're sure he will come . . . the girl is there?"

"She lives there." Danzig waved his hand. "Do not worry yourself." He finished the cigarette and lit another. "Concentrate on the target and do not think about the man." He smiled. "It is none of your business anyway. Tomorrow you will be out of Europe."

Rankin nodded. A good job; ten thousand American dollars and a ticket to New York. All he had to do was kill one man. He glanced at Danzig again. "Who is he?"

Danzig shrugged. "His name is Gerd Helbing. He is a high German official. Now forget the name."

Rankin's mouth turned down. He had heard of the man. He put the package on the table and began to unwrap it. "Why didn't you save the money and shoot him yourself?" He smiled to show it was a joke.

Danzig puffed and shrugged. "I cannot shoot straight enough. You are the expert. I would hit his arm or his knee and he would get away. It would be a calamity."

"What is he doing here in Paris?"

"I told you, he comes to visit his cupcake. She takes his mind off his work."

"Cupcake." Rankin chuckled. He pulled on a pair of thin gloves and took the rifle from the wrapping. It was in three parts, which he assembled deftly. He examined the five shining cartridges and loaded the weapon. He'd practiced three days with the rifle, getting the feel of it. He was an expert shot—when he was sober—and Danzig had insisted he stay sober. It was another thing about Danzig that annoyed him. He patted the money in his pocket and moved the table to the window. "Where is the ticket?"

Danzig took it from his overcoat pocket and handed it over. Rankin studied it: one-way to New York from Paris. All in order. He put it with the money. Danzig dropped the cigarette and lit another.

Dragging the chair to the table, Rankin sat and rested both elbows on it, cradling the rifle. He looked along the sights he'd already adjusted. It was ninety-two feet, Danzig said, from the window to the door across the street. The German was a dead man.

Rankin relaxed and looked at his watch. "What if he doesn't come?"

"He will come." Danzig blew smoke. "She is expecting him. Are your fingers cold?"

"No, I'm fine." He felt very good; not a tremor. The job would be over in a few minutes, then Danzig would drop him at the hotel and he'd be in the airport restaurant for breakfast. Danzig would go back into the woodwork, or wherever he came from, and that would be it. Piece of cake, as the Brits said.

Danzig craned his neck. "He will arrive in a Mercedes, of course. When he gets out and goes to the door, you will shoot."

Rankin sighed. "I know when to shoot, for chrissakes."

"And you will not miss."

"Jesus, Danzig, you're nervous as a hooker in church."

Danzig grunted. He dropped the cigarette butt on the floor and pulled out the pack.

Rankin stared at the street, thinking about home. A dozen years since he'd seen the States. Were any of the old hangouts still there?

"When he comes I will lift the window," Danzig said.

"Yes." They had gone over this enough times but Danzig was a nut on detail. He must be a German. Rankin watched Danzig fiddle with the cigarette and drop it, still lighted. The guy was shaky as Lucifer near the holy water. No wonder Danzig couldn't do this job himself.

He thought about Lisbon. He had worked in the embassy for two years, and lived with Isobel for one. Man! What a girl she had been! Then he'd been cashiered for drinking. That was his problem, alcohol. He was okay when he was sober, but a few drinks—

"A Mercedes," Danzig said stiffly.

It was the car. It slowed, then stopped in front of the doorway. Danzig fumbled the window up, pulled the curtains aside and stared at Rankin. "Get ready."

"I am."

"It's him!" Danzig hissed. He held a pair of small binocs to his eyes. "The car door's opening. . . ."

Looking over the sights, Rankin watched the door open. A tall man in a homburg and dark suit got out and leaned down to say something to the driver.

"That's him—that's him—shoot—shoot!"

Rankin took up the trigger slack. "You're sure it's the guy?"

Danzig swore in German.

"All right." Rankin was like ice. He centered the front sight and paused. He wanted the man to step forward just a little . . . just a step. He could not see the man's face. Helbing turned toward the door and Rankin centered the sights on the man's back, just where the heart would be. He began squeezing. Beside him Danzig was making curious hissing and squeaking noises.

Rankin didn't know when the rifle fired—until the butt slammed against his shoulder and the sharp crack of sound filled the room. He saw Helbing jerk and pitch forward, crumpling to the walkway. The man had died instantly.

The Mercedes had moved off. Someone along the street shouted and the driver braked hard. Rankin could hear the sounds clearly as he got up, leaving the rifle on the table. Danzig closed the window. The police could have the rifle, for all the good it would do them.

"Let's get outa here," Rankin said. A passerby was bending over the downed man. Another stared at the buildings across the street. Danzig peeked through the curtains. "I must make sure he is dead."

"He's dead as a plank." Rankin went to the door. "Come on."

Danzig saw another man appear. They turned the body over. Rankin was right. Helbing was dead; he saw the face

clearly in the binoculars. He could hear shouts and commotion. In a moment someone would guess where the shot
had come from.

"Come on!" Rankin snapped.

"Yes." Danzig was satisfied. "You did very well." He
crossed the room and nodded. Rankin opened the door.

As Rankin stepped into the hall, Danzig extended his
arm with the Walther and shot him four times in the back.

# Chapter Two

*Frankfurt on Main...*

The office of Undercover Operations in Frankfurt, Germany, looked to be an ordinary factory building on the outskirts of the city. "It probably fooled no one," Carol Jenner said. "But it's roomy and bug free."

She had been assigned from Fort Bragg to monitor one particular operation— and *only* one—which to her was like having a paid vacation.

She faced Mark Stone, Hog Wiley and Terry Loughlin in a small, brick-lined office that at one time had been part of a laboratory. "I asked you three here on suspicion," she said.

"Suspicion of what?" Stone asked.

"Trouble. If my suspicions were proved to be groundless... you'd have had a nice trip."

"Unfortunately...," said Loughlin.

"You're right. Unfortunately, *I* was right. There is trouble. I was a prophet." She shook out a cigarette and tapped it. "We don't know just how much trouble there is *yet.*" She stressed the "yet." "But I think the first act has begun. Two days ago Gerd Helbing was assassinated in Paris."

"Helbing was a German," Stone said. "Are you saying the French killed him?"

"No. He was in Paris to see a trade exhibit—that's the official line. Actually he had a mistress there. He was shot in front of her apartment. He was a victim of terrorists."

"How do you know?"

"We have an informer in their group. They're German terrorists. They have an elite squad led by a man called Karl Neff. We are certain one of that squad killed Helbing or caused him to be killed."

"Why?"

She lit the cigarette and blew smoke. "For several reasons. Helbing was a highly placed German official who had unusual talents. He was an organizational genius, a man almost impossible to replace. With him gone, the German government is certain to fumble and delay, and any sort of screwup plays into the terrorists' hands."

Hog Wiley yawned. "This here's all very nice, honey, but what the hell do we give a damn about what happens to the German government? They ain't high on my Christmas list."

"The second reason is"—she spoke directly to Hog—"Helbing was responsible for organizing our own secretary of state's visit to Germany. Our people in Germany are reporting rumors of a planned terrorist act against him. *That's* what this is all about."

Hog smiled at her. "Well why didn't you say so?"

Carol sighed and shook her head. "Now that you know the main facts, I'll turn you over to one of our men, Hans Meydel. He knows Karl Neff from way back."

Stone said, "Why doesn't the State Department cancel the secretary's visit?"

"And give in to rumors?" Carol made a face. "Besides, the visit has been on the books for a year. To postpone it again would cause a rift. And another reason, the secretary is determined to go through with it, come hell or high water."

Loughlin asked, "When do we see Meydel?"

"In the morning. You came in as tourists; please act like tourists." She looked hard at Hog, who gave her his best wide-eyed innocent stare.

Stone said, "No one knows we're here, do they?"

Carol sighed again. "Things leak out. God knows how, so be careful and please stay out of trouble."

Stone nodded. He knew his men could lay low; they had

done it plenty of times in Nam, on rescue missions in P.O.W. slave camps. Now, they did jobs for the government. Their home base was Fort Bragg, but the actual rescue missions could take them anywhere on the globe.

There had been others on Mark Stone's team, but the core was always the same: Terrance Loughlin and Hog Wiley, two men he trusted without question. Loughlin was a former commando of the British Special Air Services, a rough outfit. He was big, rugged and unflappable. He could come out of a fight with every hair in place.

Hog Wiley was just the opposite. He was huge, with a mane of hair, seldom combed. Unpolished and powerful, Hog was an asskicker from East Texas and proud of it. And, most important of all, he was a tiger in a fight.

They had been assigned rooms in the nearby Garr Hotel, which boasted a restaurant and bar run by an American from New Jersey. Carol Jenner had made the reservations, secure in the knowledge that the Gaar was the least likely place in all of Germany for the team to find trouble.

Karl Neff was all smiles. He embraced Danzig and called for wine. "The American gave you no trouble?" was his first question.

"He thought no farther than the money and the airline ticket." Danzig took them out of his overcoat pocket and handed them over. He laid the Walther pistol on a sideboard. "I had no chance to get rid of this."

"We will see to it," Neff said. "You have done well, my friend." He was a tall man who had the look of an aristocrat, a thin, sharp, chiseled face with flat planes. His eyes were deepset and dark; he was clean shaven and dressed always in a dark suit. He looked anything but a terrorist, or the popular idea of one.

He poured out the wine another man brought them, and he and Danzig clinked glasses and drank. "Now," Karl said, "you must leave us. Go back to Germany at once. I will be there in a few days."

"No one knows I—"

Karl held up his hand. "See no one, talk to none of your

sources. Go at once. We take no chances. Someone may have seen you with the American, Rankin."

"Very well." Danzig finished the wine and put the glass down. He went to the door.

"Do not use the telephone," Karl stressed. "You must disappear into thin air."

Danzig nodded. He turned the knob and went out.

Karl snapped his fingers and Conrad Banner came into the room, a questioning look on his flat face.

"That was Danzig," Karl said. "Go after him. See that he returns to Frankfurt at once."

"You do not trust him?" Banner was short and stocky with thinning hair and a stub of nose.

"I trust him—that far." Karl held up a hand with two fingers spread. "If he does not go at once or meets with anyone, get rid of him. We cannot jeopardize the mission because of one man."

"I understand." Banner hurried out.


The murder of Gerd Helbing had caused a sensation in all the media. Speculation was rife—what did it mean? Surely it was not the act of a jealous suitor. The girl in the case, Helbing's mistress, Odile Buchon, was characterized as a model, an actress and a woman of pleasure. A photograph of her, dug up by an enterprising reporter, showed her dressed in a skimpy swimsuit, revealing more front acreage than many men saw of their wives for the first year.

The police escorted her to interrogation rooms at once, but got very little from her. Yes, she had known Gerd was arriving that day, but she had said nothing to anyone about it—how the assassin had known, she could not say.

She said the same thing to the television crews, then her lawyer whisked her off.

In Stone's room at the Gaar, the three saw the news reports on television. Hog said, "Great pair of tits. I like 'em when they waggle like that."

Loughlin sighed. "A man died at her door. Does that mean nothing to you?"

"Sure. I'd die for a pair of tits like that too, any day of

the week. Are they sayin' she was a hooker?"

"Probably was."

Stone said, "The German was killed by a single shot. That means the shooter was an expert. He knew the exact range."

"The cops say it was Webster Rankin, a guy who used to work for the American embassy in Lisbon." Loughlin lit a cigarette. "They're trying to connect the U.S. government with the shooting."

"I guess that's always good copy. A certain class of idiots will believe it."

"Who was the other guy?" Hog asked. "The guy who shot the shooter?"

Stone smiled. "Now you've asked the sixty-four-thousand-dollar question. Let's see what Meydel has to say about that."

# Chapter Three

Hans Meydel was a thin, almost skinny, little man wearing thick glasses. He had a dome-shaped head that gave him the look of someone from outer space, and he had a prissy way of speaking, though his English was excellent, with a British accent.

They met him in the same brick-lined room. He came in with an attaché case, put it down, smiled at them and asked who was who.

"This is Loughlin, that's Hog Wiley and I'm Stone."

"Ahh. Good to meet you, gentlemen." He put his hands in his pockets as he faced them. They sprawled in armchairs. He said, "We have a good deal more information now about the shooting. It was definitely done by Webster Rankin. He was well known as an expert with firearms. We have an informant on the other side and he tells us he is certain that Rankin was hired to do the shooting by Neff's terrorist organization. You have heard of Karl Neff?"

Stone nodded.

"Good. This is the first time Neff's group has operated in a foreign country—that we know of. We think it was done deliberately in hope of embarrassing the United States."

Stone said, "You mean by hiring an American to do the shooting."

"Exactly. Our informant says they had any number of men who could have done it. Webster Rankin worked for the American embassy in Lisbon, as the media has said.

He was there for two years and was fired for drinking. He was an alcoholic."

Loughlin asked, "Did he have any connection with the terrorist group?"

"None whatsoever, that we can determine at this point. He was apparently hired by them and possibly he did not know who was doing the hiring. He may not even have known who he killed."

"So there is only a tenuous connection between Rankin and the man who hired him—presumably the man who killed him." Stone frowned. "Not much of a lead."

"No it isn't. We have feelers out as do the police, but I'm afraid they'll turn up nothing. We have to assume that the killer is long gone."

Stone said, "Carol Jenner mentioned her suspicions— the reason she asked us to come here. She said she thinks this killing is the first act to something."

"Yes. We are very apprehensive about the visit of the American secretary of state."

"We don't do guard work," Hog said.

Meydel shook his head. "No one expects you to. He will be well guarded." He smiled at them. "We want you to bring in Karl Neff . . . and his gang."

They stared at him. Stone said, "You want us to do what the police have not been able to do for years?"

Meydel kept smiling. "You come very well recommended."

"So did Helbing's hooker," Hog said.

Meydel drew up a chair and sat down. "You are able to do what the police cannot do—they have rules and regulations. You three are guerrilla fighters—like the terrorists."

"How many of them are there?"

"We don't know exactly, their members change, but Neff's group probably numbers eight to ten . . . dedicated killers." Meydel took an envelope from an inside coat pocket. He opened it and drew out a photograph. "This is Karl Neff—about ten years ago. He probably hasn't changed much." He handed the photo to Stone.

Stone looked at a thin face with hooded eyes. He looked like a member of the German general staff. Neff would not have been out of place with von Hindenburg. He handed the photo to Hog.

Meydel said, "Neff is a very well-educated man. He was once in business—contracting—where I first met him. I was a building inspector at the time."

"He is an ex-soldier?"

"Yes, in a commando unit. After his discharge he went into contracting but did not stay in it. He and a group of his soldier comrades banded together and began to deal in black-market goods and drugs. Karl's group is now a part of a larger terrorist organization, but his particular group is elite. They are the dangerous ones. They are hyenas."

Stone said, "Why would they want to kill the secretary of state?"

"Oh, we don't think they want to kill him. Neff's group does everything for money. We think they intend to hold him for ransom."

"My word!" Loughlin said. "They think big!"

Meydel shrugged. "That's our guess, of course. They may do either—if they get the chance."

"Too bad the secretary won't change his mind."

Meydel nodded. "We've tried everything. Your government has tried everything." He shrugged again. "So we sent for you."


Neff did not go along on the raid. He was in his sixties; he would leave the firefights to younger men—but he would plan them. His second in command, Johann Dicot, was fully capable of leading the group.

There were seven men in the truck, all dressed in camouflage fatigues with blackened faces. It was one o'clock in the morning when they arrived near the general's base home, having easily passed two lightly guarded checkpoints. Dicot wore major's leaves and was familiar with the drill. The closed-up truck was not stopped, except for a brief moment at each point.

Nothing had disturbed the tranquillity of the base for months and the daily routine had become dull, so Dicot had reported to Karl Neff. It was exactly the right time to attempt their plan.

There was no guard stationed at the house itself, but a regular MG jeep made hourly rounds. It held four men, two of whom got out and walked around the house with flashlights.

They could be seen, Dicot said, half a mile away.

He parked the truck a hundred yards from the general's house, beside a long low warehouse shed . . . and waited for the jeep to make its round.

When it came and went, the men piled out and Dicot sent them to the house, half to the back, one man remaining with the truck. He was a dark, lithe man in his late twenties. He wore a Walther on his hip and carried a burglar's jimmy which he gave to Ernst, a man with burglar training. Ernst had spent time behind walls for that crime.

One of the front windows yielded easily to the crowbar; the weather was mild and shutters had not yet been put up. Dicot slipped into the darkened house behind Ernst, with Horst at his heels. The other team would stay vigilant at the far end of the house—and not enter unless there was trouble. The general and his wife were expected to be alone.

But they were not.

Dicot had a plan of the house, bought from a soldier on the post who had been inside. It showed three bedrooms upstairs; the master bedroom was on the east side at the head of the stairs. As he headed for the staircase he saw the light.

Instantly he halted and Horst ran into him, dropping a flashlight.

A youngish man appeared in the doorway of the lighted room. "Is that you, Dad?"

Dicot swore under his breath.

There was no possibility of answering the man. Dicot motioned to Ernst. A glittering knife appeared in Ernst's hand. He ran forward four or five steps and threw the knife. It struck the man in the doorway. The man yelped and fell back into the room.

Instantly two more men appeared in the doorway, one with a short rifle that barked at them. Dicot went to his knees and fired the Walther. He saw one man whirl away;

the other dropped his rifle, grabbing an arm that spurted blood. Turning, Dicot motioned to the stairs. He was swearing under his breath.

Horst ran up the steps, paused halfway up and fired his pistol. Shots came from above, and Dicot ran back in time to see an older man crumple at the head of the stairs. A woman began to shriek from a bedroom.

Ernst ran up past Horst, kicked a .45 automatic away and grabbed the man. It was General Massey. Dicot recognized him from the photos. He yelled, "Bring him down. Is he hurt bad?"

"He's got one through his leg," Ernst said.

Horst ran up and helped. Between them they got the general down, his leg leaving a bloody trail on the steps. As they reached the main floor, Victor and Otto came running through the house, having heard the shots.

"Get him out to the truck! Hurry!" Dicot opened the front door of the house. Had the general sounded an alarm? He gave a quick look around; nothing moved. He ran after the others and opened the rear door of the truck. They shoved the wounded man in and Horst clambered in after him.

"Bind up the leg!" Dicot shouted. He ran for the driver's seat. As he started the engine and put the vehicle in gear, he heard the first alarm sounds, a piercing whistle, echoed by another. Beside him, Ernst swore terrible oaths and reloaded his pistol.

When they approached the first check station, two men ran out, waving their arms. Ernst said, "Don't stop—"

Dicot growled in reply, trod on the accelerator and smashed through the striped gate, hearing half a dozen voices yelling. Lights went on, bathing the area as if by the sun. Ernst was swearing steadily.

As they approached the second check gate Ernst leaned out and fired a burst. The guards scattered, but shots slammed into the side of the truck as they smashed through the flimsy gate. One shot cracked by them and left a hole in the windshield.

Then Dicot made a sharp turn onto the highway and

they were out! No more shots came after them.

He took a deep breath and turned on the lights.


Stone and his men were called to the Operations building very early the next morning to be met by Carol Jenner and little Hans Meydel in the now-familiar brick-lined room.

Stone said, "What's up?"

"Last night—really early this morning," she replied, "only a few hours ago, General Massey was kidnapped off the army base."

Loughlin was astonished. "Off the army base! How could that happen?"

"It did. Half a dozen men in fatigues, led by a man purporting to be a major, did the job."

"They knew exactly where to go," broke in Meydel.

"Yes. And they killed the general's son and one other man, and wounded a third. They broke into the general's house—we think either he or one of the raiders was wounded—bloodstains. General Massey managed to sound the alarm, but the response was too slow to help. The raiders got away."

"The general's wife?"

"She wasn't harmed."

"Anything else missing?"

Carol shook her head. "No report yet."

"Bad show," Loughlin said. "What do you think they'll do next?"

Meydel looked at him. "We expect a ransom note," he said.

Stone scratched his chin, frowning at Carol. "Is this part of your suspicion syndrome?"

"I think so. If Hans is right and they ask for money, it's probably Karl Neff's group."

"You said we had an informer in that group some-where."

"We do, and we hope to hear from him. Of course he'll have a problem getting news out to us at this time—as you can imagine. The slightest suspicious move on anyone's part . . ." She shrugged.

Both the German government and the Americans were pooling their resources, Carol told them, and a massive manhunt was getting under way. The general's capture was international news and the American news media were making a real fuss.

"The big brass is grateful for the police help," Meydel said, "but when it comes down to it, they want you three to get the general out. As soon as we know where he is. . . ."

# Chapter Four

Dicot drove to a warehouse in the industrial section of Frankfurt. A man was waiting at the gate and rolled it back when the approaching truck gave a quick headlight signal. As the gate closed, Dicot drove down a long dark side of the building and entered a downward ramp to a basement. Another door closed behind the truck and lights went on.

He parked the truck, heading in to a wall, and they piled out. Two men carried the fuming general. "Where the hell are you taking me?"

"Be quiet, General," Dicot said. "You will be told all you need to know."

"Kidnappers!"

Dicot motioned to Ernst. "Shut him up." He walked away. Ernst backhanded the white-haried man.

They half carried him through a door, down a short hall and into a room that Dicot said was soundproofed. "Yell all you please, General. No one will hear you."

They tied him to a large wooden armchair and Dicot looked at the man's leg. The bullet had smashed the bone and the general was obviously in great pain. The wound was roughly bound up and only seeping blood. It was good enough.

"What do you want?" the general said through clenched teeth.

Dicot shrugged. "Money. What did you think?"

19

• • •

Carol had a slip of paper and read from it. "The only clue the police have so far about the Helbing shooting concerns smoked cigarettes left at the scene."

Stone said, "Do they know who smoked them?"

She smiled. "It was not Rankin. Saliva tests rule him out."

Loughlin put his feet up on a chair. "I take it the man's name was not on the cigarette butts?"

"Unfortunately, no. But the man who smoked them was a chain-smoker . . . at least during that time."

"Nervous," Stone said. "He knew what he would have to do as soon as Helbing was dead."

Hog asked, "What about the girl with the ti—er—the mistress?"

"Odile Buchon? She is being watched. The police are still wondering how the killers knew Helbing was coming to that address . . . at that precise time. So far they've gotten nothing from the girl. She has said only that Helbing came when he wanted, often without phoning first." She made a face. "It does not sound reasonable."

Hog said, "Maybe we ought to go see her."

Carol studied him with a glint in her eyes. "Why do I have the feeling you're more interested in the girl than in what she has to say?"

Stone and Loughlin laughed as Hog drew himself up. "I oughta wash your mind out with soap, honey. Them are terrible thoughts."

"Terribly close to the mark, I think."

Stone said, "So the police suspect she was an accomplice?"

"It's possible. But the French police are very close-mouthed. They tell us very little. They have said they're watching her." Carol shrugged again. "The German cops are not happy. After all, it was a German who was shot."

"And now it's an American who was kidnapped."

Carol shook her head . . . and the telephone rang. She crossed the room and said, "Hello . . ." into the instrument.

Her expression changed as she listened. Then she said, "Thank you," and hung up. She looked at him. "A note was delivered to the American ambassador five minutes ago. It asks one million dollars American for General Massey."

"A bloody lot of money!" Loughlin said.

"What else?" Stone asked

"That's it. Instructions will follow. The note was delivered by a boy on a bicycle. He says he got the note from a man he'd never seen before. The man gave him some money and showed him where to go. They're getting a description from the boy now."

"It won't be much help," Stone said.

"I suppose not."

"Are they going to pay it?" Loughlin asked.

She shook her head. "I don't know."

They stayed in the Operations building, reading, eating and sleeping, for the next five hours. Then Carol called them together again, with a new urgency in her voice.

"We've received word from the informant."

Loughlin rubbed his hands together. Stone said, "Tell us . . ."

"General Massey is being held in an empty warehouse in the industrial district. He is on the second floor in a soundproofed room, and he is wounded, a shot in the leg. He has not received medical attention."

"Where is the warehouse?"

"Someone will point it out to you." She looked at her watch. "It's eight P.M. now. When do you want to go?"

"We'll be ready in half an hour." Stone looked at the others, who nodded.

Loughlin asked, "Has anyone a plan of the warehouse?"

"No. We know nothing about it. We might be able to get plans from the owner, but it would take time to find out who he is —" She made a face. "It might take days."

"We got to play it by ear then," Hog said. "We done that before."

They examined their equipment, reloaded pistols and Uzi submachine guns and slipped into camouflage fatigues and black berets. Carol left and came back with a slim young man she introduced as Otto. He would go with them to point out the warehouse. Then he would disappear.

"He is not a warrior," she told them. "He is only an embassy messenger."

"Don't sweat it, honey," Hog said. "I wasn't allus a warrior m'self."

"Yes," Loughlin agreed. "He was once a Bengal tiger."

Danzig went from Karl Neff's hideout to his apartment to pack a bag. He let himself in with a key and was mildly surprised to find Joanny there. They had been living together for more than a year.

He went into the bedroom and pulled a bag off a shelf and opened a bureau drawer. Joanny stood in the doorway. "What are you doing?"

"I have to go out of town for a few days."

"Were you going to tell me about it?"

"Of course. I'm telling you now."

She crossed her arms. "What is this about, Danzig?"

"Nothing important. I have to go—"

"So you said. But why?"

"Business." He stopped to pull out a pack and select a cigarette. He gave her a quick smile. She and her brother were just alike, inquisitive as hell. And him a policeman.

"What kind of business?"

He piled underwear and shirts into the bag. "Just ordinary business. Gott, woman, I'll be back in a few days." He lit the cigarette.

"You're so damned secretive, Danzig. You always were."

He glowered at her. Gott, women were difficult. How glad he was he wasn't married to this one! She was good ass in bed, but a pain in the ass now. He clicked the lock on the bag and went to the door.

"When will you be back?"

"I told you—in a few days. I've got to hurry."

"Will you telephone me?"

"Of course." He gave her a quick one on the cheek and hurried to the door again. "I'll be back before you know it." He went out and slammed the door.

She made herself a supper when it got dark, then sat in front of the television. According to the news broadcast they were still looking for the man who had assassinated Gerd Helbing. He was described as a chain-smoker.

She blinked at the set. Danzig was a chain-smoker. No—no, it could not be him. The announcer said it was the opinion of the police that the killer had probably left the country.

Joanny looked at the door. Had he left the country? Was that his "business"?

She stared at the television screen, hearing nothing. What did Danzig do for a living? She had never known. She got up and drew on a coat. Letting herself out of the apartment, she went down the stairs to the street and along it three blocks to her brother's house. When she reached it she stood outside, looking at the lighted windows. Should she go in—should she tell him her suspicions? She had no proof at all. . . .

As she debated with herself, a group of noisy children came along the street and she went up the steps and knocked on the door. Her brother, in shirtsleeves, opened it.

"Joanny! What is it?" He pulled her in.

She went in, doffed the coat and sat in the chair he indicated. His wife was out, he said, and would be back shortly. "What is it? Are you and Danzig having trouble?"

She took a long breath and told him what she feared.


The young man told them everyone called him O.T. He wore a gray sweatshirt, dark pants and tennis shoes. As soon as he delivered them, he said, he was going to a ball game.

He had a small car. Hog and Loughlin struggled to get in the back; Stone sat in front with him. O. T. asked no questions; he drove them across town, very careful to obey traffic laws. Stone had considered having the boy wait for them and drive them back, but decided against it. It might put the lad in jeopardy unnecessarily. Loughlin could easily liberate a car for them—he was an expert at it—and they would leave it where it could be found in the morning.

They entered the industrial section and the lad drove more slowly. He would drive past the building, he said, not stopping. There was a good chance traffic was watched. Stone agreed.

When they turned into the street O.T. said, "That's it on the right, the big, dark building, just beyond the row of small brick buildings."

Stone examined it as they passed. There was a large, high entrance gate, mostly wire. He could see into a dark yard. There was a small gatehouse, and the link fence, about eight feet high, continued along the street, turning at the next building.

Then they were past. O.T. turned the next corner and stopped.

"Thanks for the ride," Stone said, getting out. "Forget you saw us."

"I was never here," O.T. said cheerfully. When Hog and Loughlin got out and closed the door he waved and put the car in gear.

Loughlin had brought along a pair of wire cutters, having been told about the fence. When they went back to the corner of the fence, and along it a few yards, it was the work of a moment to cut a hole large enough to step through.

"I doubt if they'll have many guards out," Stone said. "They depend on secrecy. They probably have a couple of escape routes." He led them around a row of sheds that were across from the building proper. The unlighted yard between the sheds and the building was wide, with no cover at all. When the building was in operation the yard was probably crammed with trucks and other vehicles.

They could go around the yard but it might take a half hour. Stone was about to step out to cross it, when Loughlin tugged at his sleeve and pointed. There was a flare of light at the gatehouse as someone lit a cigarette.

Stone said, "Shit."

Hog Wiley screwed a silencer to the muzzle of his pistol. "Not a good idea to leave somebody in our rear anyways." He moved silently toward the gatehouse.

# Chapter Five

Odile Buchon sat at her dressing table, combing out her tawny hair. She was vastly annoyed. The French police had interrogated her for hours on several occasions, not bothering to conceal their opinion that she was implicated in the death of Gerd Helbing.

Odile smiled. She had done well. They could prove nothing.

She had not gone to him; Helbing had come to her. He came when he pleased and most of the time, she had told them, she had not known in advance when he would arrive.

None of that was true. He had telephoned her each time, but they could not prove that either. Or she would be in jail.

On the day he died, she had known to the minute when he would arrive. She had insisted on his telephoning, making up a story about having to arrange her time to see him.

And then she had told Karl.

And now it was all over. She would no longer have to accept him in her bed. He had not been a bad lover, but he had been unimaginative and not quite as durable as she would have liked. She preferred men who lasted upwards of an hour . . . or more. When she went to bed with a man for money it did not matter, and it really had not mattered with Gerd, except that the affair had lasted much longer than Karl had said it would.

"It is politics," Karl had said. "Fuck him a few more times."

So now it was over, but she could not leave. The police were watching her. It was very, very annoying.

Wiley circled around, moving behind the sheds to a point behind the gatehouse where there was no window. When he stepped close to the enclosure he could hear the man's radio playing softly. It must be lonely duty. Hog peered at his watch; it was exactly ten o'clock . . . and some instinct kept him from moving around to the gatehouse door.

He was surprised to hear a greeting in German. Someone had approached and he'd not heard the footsteps. Two men were talking inside the tiny house, then one said: *"Wiedersehen,"* and Hog heard his boots on the gravel. The guard had just been changed.

Hog smiled; his luck was still holding. Mentally he patted Lady Luck on the ass, waited till the footsteps receded, then moved to the doorway. The new guard, a smallish, dark-haired man, saw him instantly and pulled a revolver. Hog shot him twice, closed the door and hurried back to the others. "Go."

Stone nodded and led out across the yard.

At the building they paused, examining it. It was built of blocks of some gray stone; the windows were high up and barred. There was a loading ramp to their left and a wide doorway to the right, with the door closed. It was a deserted building, but it was well locked up.

Loughlin clambered up onto the loading ramp. "There's a door here. . . ." It was locked but he took out his knife and began to cut away around the lock. In a few minutes he had bared the lock and the door swung open.

They moved inside and closed the door. They were in a vast room with only a faint light filtering in from the high windows. It was very quiet. They could hardly hear the ordinary sounds of the city in the distance.

"The second floor," Stone said softly. "Look for stairs."

Hog pointed. "Over there."

The room had huge concrete pillars at intervals, and

they found a staircase beside one of them. Stone took the lead, climbing the stairs and cradling his Uzi. Halfway up he halted, motioning them. There were noises from above —then a man appeared and started down the steps in a hurry, his head down.

He looked up and saw them; his eyes widened and his mouth opened to yell. Hog shot him with the silenced pistol and the body rolled down to them and sprawled facedown, arms extended, like a rag doll.

Stone ran up the stairs quickly with Hog and Loughlin at his heels. Men were talking very close by . . . and one of them saw him as he reached a point where he could see over the top step. The man gave a yell and went for his gun. Stone fired a burst with the Uzi; the man crumpled and a row of holes was stitched across a door thirty feet away.

At the top of the stairs was an area that had been offices. Facing them were half a dozen doors, most standing open, with lights on in two of them. Men spilled from the rooms and AK-47 rounds smashed the wall behind Stone and his men.

Stone dropped to the floor, firing the Uzi. Hog and Loughlin sprayed the doors. Someone yelled and a door slammed. Then it was silent.

Stone got to his knees cautiously. There were five bodies lying in various attitudes in front of them. The element of surprise had paid off again. The terrorists hadn't been able to get their weapons into action fast enough. He looked around. "Anybody hurt?"

Hog shook his head and Loughlin said, "One or two of 'em got away down that hall." He pointed to his left. "They probably thought there were twenty of us."

Hog reloaded the Uzi. "Look in them doors, neighbor."

Loughlin opened doors cautiously along the hallway. In the third room, a small square dark cubicle, they found General Massey, tied to a heavy wooden armchair. He was unconscious, his head hanging down.

Stone cut the heavy cords that bound him and they lowered him to the floor. He looked frail and white, his face very lined and drawn into a grimace. His leg was dark with dried blood, and twisted inward.

"Jesus! He needs a doc," Hog said.

"There's a telephone in the next room," Loughlin replied. "I'll call Carol."

"Tell 'er to get 'er ass in gear," Hog said. "This here gent ain't going to last."

Loughlin hurried out. Stone said,"We haven't a thing to give him. The poor son of a bitch must be out of his head with the pain of that wound."

"You want we should carry him down?"

"Better not move him. Let the bearers get him."

Hog nodded. "I'll go down and open the gate." He went out and listened at the door as Loughlin related to Carol Jenner what they had run into. When Loughlin hung up, he went down the stairs with Hog.

Near the bottom they heard someone running across the concrete floor, the steps coming toward them. Loughlin halted, raising the Uzi—and saw the girl. He put out his arm, pushing Hog's weapon down. The girl was with a tall, well-dressed man.

With a shock, he recognized her!

At the same instant she saw him, and recognized him— he could see it in her eyes. She was not armed, dressed in black, her hair severely bound back. She said, *"Terry!"*

In the next moment the man grabbed her and pushed her through a door and slammed it behind them.

Loughlin still stood, staring for several heartbeats, then he stumbled down the last few steps as Hog ran to the door and tried to open it. It was a metal door painted brown, and the man had locked it on the other side. Hog jumped to one side and fired a burst with the Uzi at the lock, but with no luck.

He turned then and looked at Loughlin. "She knew you, neighbor."

"Yes . . ."

"Something you ain't told us." Hog looked at him curiously.

"I knew her a long time ago." He turned away. "Let's go open the gate."

The German police arrived at almost the same time as the ambulance Carol Jenner had ordered. The police captain was a suave black-haired man in a business suit. He gave orders crisply and the building was surrounded at once and a search begun of every inch. American MPs arrived and watched the general being placed in the ambulance, then they took off with the ambulance at high speed toward the hospital.

Stone, Hog and Loughlin were taken aside by the captain and an assistant, who had a notepad. The captain's name was Brockhof, he told them; their names were noted on the assistant's pad.

Brockhof was not pleased that they had entered the building and caused the deaths of five men, terrorists or not. "I will not have this kind of thing in my city!"

Stone was polite, referring the captain to his superiors, and Brockhof began to simmer down, especially when he was told that the dead men were undoubtedly part of Karl Neff's group. Anything that whittled down that group was to the good.

The search turned up very little. There was food, a television set, a truck in the basement and various weapons, including grenades, but no papers or letters. The bodies were taken away to be identified later. General Massey would be questioned when he was able to speak.

Brockhof let them go finally and they returned to the Operations building to make their report to Carol Jenner, with Meydel standing by.

The report was routine until Loughlin said, "One more thing—I recognized one of them."

Carol looked up in astonishment. "What!"

"He got girls all over the goddamn world," Hog said.

"What girl?" Stone asked. "There was no—"

"When we went down to open the gate." Loughlin took a long breath. "We came across a man and a girl. The man was Karl Neff. He looks just like his photo. The girl was someone I knew from the SAS. Her name is Eva Ullman."

"How well did you know her?" Carol asked.

"We were lovers," Loughlin said.

# Chapter Six

"I'll be damned!" Carol said. "You three never cease to amaze me. Did you speak to her?"

Loughlin shook his head.

Hog said, "She said his name." He mimicked her. "Terry..."

"Knock it off," Stone said. He looked at Loughlin. "Let's have the dirt. Tell us all."

The Britisher took a long breath. "We worked together on a few missions when I was with the SAS. And on one of them she got in a burst that saved my bacon. I owe her a good one. I was badly wounded and she took out one of the bad guys before he could fire a kill shot."

Carol said, "And now she's a terrorist?"

"She was with Karl Neff, but she was unarmed. It was impossible to know if she was one of them or a prisoner. He shoved her through the door—"

"That's right," Hog said. "It woulda been tough to hit him and not touch her."

"Did Neff get a good look at you two?"

"The light was poor, but yes, I think so," Loughlin replied.

Carol asked, "How long since you've seen her?"

"Years," Loughlin said. "Since long before I hitched a ride with these two." He indicated Hog and Stone.

"And you've never heard from her in the interval?"

"No. Never. I was astonished to see her tonight."

Hog chuckled. "He stood there like a goddamn wooden Indian, staring at her."

"I never got a chance to repay her," Loughlin said in a small voice.

Carol said, "We'll have to put out feelers and see what we can learn about her . . . Eva Ullman? She's probably changed her name. Do you think it's likely she'd team up with terrorists?"

Loughlin shook his head. "I can't imagine it."

"All right," Carol said. "Get some sleep and stay under cover. The German police are unhappy with you because they weren't called in soon enough. Don't give them any opportunity to show you who's boss. Captain Brockhof seems like a nice guy but he wears stainless-steel underpants."

"You're cute," Hog said, touching her nose. "How do you know?"

She laughed. "Get out of here."

Later, Carol arranged to have them assigned quarters in the Operations building, making it less likely that Brockhof's men could touch them. Ordinary police might be forced to work with foreign undercover people, but it was next to impossible to make them like it. Cops were jealous of their own bailiwick.

Loughlin was troubled, saying, "I'm sure Eva was not with Neff of her own free will."

Hog said, "You only saw her a few seconds."

"Maybe so, but I had the strong feeling . . . And I owe her something."

"You're letting it get to you," Stone warned. "We have no idea where she is. Until Carol's sources turn up something we can get our teeth into—"

"I'm going to have a look for myself," Loughlin said. "I speak the language. Maybe I can scare something up."

"You ain't goin' alone," Hog said.

Stone frowned. "What do you think you can accomplish?"

"I don't know," Loughlin said doggedly. "But I have to try. I—"

"I know, I know, you owe her." Stone sighed. "Okay.

Hog's right. You're not going alone." He turned as a rap came at the door.

Hog opened it and a young GI stood there with a slip of paper. "Message for Terrance Loughlin," he said.

"That's me," Hog said. "Where'd you get it?"

"It came in to the message center downstairs a few minutes ago."

"Thanks." Hog closed the door and handed the paper to Loughlin.

The Brit was surprised. "It's from Eva! It's a telephone number. I'm to call it in an hour." He glanced at his watch.

Stone looked at the paper. "D'you know her writing?"

"No . . ."

"This could be a forgery . . . a trap of some kind, if she wants to meet you."

"It would be natural for her to request a meeting."

Stone nodded. "Yes . . . so we've got to be careful as hell. Maybe she was forced to make the call."

"Maybe they leaned on her tits," Hog said, and made a face as Loughlin glared at him.

When the hour was up they went to a row of public telephones in a wide hallway. Loughlin made the call and listened to the ring. A receiver was picked up after the third ring. "Yes?"

"Eva—this is Terrance."

"Oh, Terry! I'm so glad to hear from you. You have no idea how I wanted to run and hug you!"

"How well do you know Karl Neff?"

"Not at all! Believe me, I'm not part of that gang! But I'll tell you all about it when I see you. I must hurry—"

"When will I see you?"

"Why not tonight? Do you know the city?"

"I can get a guide."

"Good. I will be at a house on the Trummer Road, number Fifty-three. It is a few miles past a shopping center, a white house with two chimneys. I will be there at eight o'clock this evening."

"All right. I'll find it."

"It will be wonderful to see you, Terry." She hung up.

He had written down the instructions. When they

showed the paper to Hans Meydel he said in surprise, "But this is in a forest! Did she tell you that?"

"No. Are you certain?"

"Of course I am. I know that area well." He went out and came back with a map, smoothing it out on a table. "Here is where we are." He penciled a circle. "Over here is the Trummer Road. You see it curves about the hills and goes nearly straight north for maybe fifty kilometers. This is the shopping center she mentioned." He circled it. "The area is all heavily wooded."

"Suspicious as hell," Hog said. "You sure it was her?"

Loughlin frowned. "I haven't heard her voice for years. It sounded like her. . . ."

Stone asked, "Couldn't it have been someone who sounded like her, but wasn't?"

Loughlin shrugged. "Yes—of course."

"Well, we'll take precautions," Stone said. "If it was someone else, setting a trap—"

Hog said, "We'll squeeze her tits till she confesses!"

Stone said, "You're getting to be a real tit man, you know it?"

"Always have been, dude. You just ain't noticed."

"I've noticed it lately."

"Well, these German tits ain't bad. I'll stick 'em up against French tits anytime."

Stone sighed. "Let's go get ready."

They cleaned and loaded weapons and got a few hours' sleep. Then Stone called Carol and told her what they needed in the way of transportation. When they joined her, she had a middle-aged man with her.

"This is Jerry Conte. He's in charge of the motor pool. Tell him what you need."

Conte was a gray-haired man who looked like a stockbroker. He was in civvies with a green sweater and a baseball cap. He nodded to them and Stone said, "We need a jeep and a motorcycle."

"For how long?"

"Probably overnight."

Conte looked from one to the other of them. "I've heard

of you guys. You went into the factory, right? You gonna
get holes in my vehicles?"

"I certainly hope not," Stone said piously. "If we get
holes in them, we might get holes in us."

"That's right," Hog added. "Then when all the red stuff
runs out, neighbor, we is finished."

Conte stared at him. "Where the hell you from?"

"Texas, for chrissakes."

The older man smiled. "Hey, me too. I was born in San
Angelo."

Hog embraced him. "God damn! We goin' to win this
here war after all!"

Conte did not have a jeep available, he said, but he
could give them a small Fiat.

"What color?"

"It's dark red. Five or six years old, but runs good. I got
half a dozen bikes. When you come down to the yard, you
take your pick."


Stone and Hog Wiley crowded into the little Fiat.
They would arrive at the house twenty minutes before
Loughlin on the bike. They would also arrive at the house
an hour before the time specified by Eva Ullman. Loughlin
would arrive, ride by and come back, looking the place
over. If it was a trap they'd think he was alone. They
hoped.

"Take your time," Stone warned. "If it's a trap they'll
expect you to be wary."

"And dumb."

Hog chuckled. "They'll figure you's hot for the chick."

"I can't imagine Eva setting me up." Loughlin shook his
head.

Stone studied his watch. "Time to go." He gave the
thumbs-up signal and they drove off.

The house was easy to find. They found a place to ditch
the Fiat half a mile from it and went on foot through the
dark woods. Hog circled the house and Stone settled down
in a patch of brush where he could see the road and the

front of the house. It was silent, only a dim light showing inside.

Several airliners went by far overhead and an owl hooted not far off. Only one car went by the road, heading for the city. It was a lonely place.

The minutes crept by. Then came the far-off sound of the motorcycle. It approached and went by at a slower pace and Stone could see Loughlin peering at the house. It passed and came back in several minutes, moving by again, even slower.

The third time he passed he moved at walking speed, as if trying to make up his mind. But he went by.

Stone eased his big body in the brush. He moved the Uzi to a more comfortable position and froze. Did he hear engines from a distance? For a second he thought they were approaching. . . . Now they had stopped, and he could no longer hear them.

Loughlin returned on the bike, and this time he turned in at the house and stopped, shutting off the engine. The stillness seemed to intensify.

Stone watched Loughlin get off the machine and approach the house steps. He was only a darker shadow in the night. He stood at the bottom of the steps, apparently listening . . . then he took the steps three at a time.

The two cars came along the road, one from each direction, at breakneck speed. One moment the night was still, the next it was roaring with sound. They must be in radio communication, is what passed through Stone's head. They raced to the house and stopped with screaming brakes, slewing sideways—and men erupted from them like magic. Powerful lights went on suddenly, making the area brighter than day.

But Loughlin was nowhere to be seen.

Stone had not seen him go. The men ran around the house to surround it, several went inside, there were shouts and orders given—then the signal came, two blasts of a whistle.

It was the signal they had agreed upon. Stone rose to one knee and raked the yard with Uzi fire. From the far side of the house Hog's weapon stuttered, and then Stone saw Loughlin. He ran between the two cars, spraying them with Uzi fire—and in a moment one car erupted in flames.

The ambushers were ambushed.

# Chapter Seven

The terrorist leader was quick. He pulled his men back, retreating toward the trees behind the house. Stone figured the guy must have no idea what or who he faced—it might even be police. It would take him a few moments to get reports . . .

Stone hurried after Loughlin. Hog came from his position, grinning from ear to ear. There were two bodies near the now-wrecked cars, and Loughlin bent over them, searching them quickly.

Stone could see at glance that the two cars were wrecked beyond repair. He said to Loughlin, "Get on the bike and get moving."

He and Hog ran down the road to the Fiat.

Carol Jenner was pacing the dark area before the Operations building gate when they returned.

"Piece of cake," Loughlin told her.

"Did you see the girl?"

He shook his head. "There was no girl there; it was only an ambush."

"Except we outfoxed 'em," Hog told her. He looked at Loughlin. "How'd you get off that porch?"

"There were men in the house. I just dived into the roses and waited till they surrounded the place. It was nothing, really."

Carol took them to the brick-lined room and sat tiredly.

"Well, it proves that this Eva person is on the other side."

"Not necessarily," Loughlin protested.

"She is the only one who could have told Karl Neff who you are."

"Maybe she was forced to tell him." He pulled some papers from his pocket. "I took these off the two bodies by the cars." He handed them to Carol.

She spread them on the table. "They're check receipts made out to Ludwig Buchinger and August Duhr . . . from the Club Heppe. They both worked at a club."

She went to the telephone and called a number. She lighted a cigarette while she waited for it to ring, then she spoke softly to someone for a minute and hung up.

"The Club Heppe," she said, "has long been suspected of being a terrorist hangout. I think we just struck pay dirt."

Captain Brockhof was very unhappy the next morning when he protested by phone to the American embassy that three German citizens had been killed the night before on Trummer Road. He suspected the killers were the same three men who had entered the factory after Karl Neff.

"Karl Neff is a terrorist," he was informed.

"I know that!"

A suave voice at the embassy said smoothly, "And have you been successful in bringing him to justice, Captain?"

Brockhof swore in German.

"Perhaps you would prefer to work with these men. They seem to be able to find Neff."

Brockhof hung up.

The suave voice called Carol Jenner. "Do your men have to ruffle the feathers of the German police quite as much as they do?"

"They do not do it purposefully, sir."

"I understand. Perhaps they could be more circumspect. . . ."

"I will tell them, sir."

"Thank you." He hung up.

• • •

General Massey was out of danger at the hospital; he had suffered shock, loss of blood from the shattered leg, and had been beaten about the head.

He had not been able to identify his assailants. He had an impression of a dark man in fatigues who had fired at him, and that was all. He had gotten off two shots with the .45 and had been able to sound the alarm—then he'd been hit. The next thing he knew he was in the hospital with no idea how he'd gotten there.

The death of his son had hit him hard also; he was seriously considering retirement.

It was another victory for the terrorists, Carol thought. They were eliminating the veterans, one by one, the people who could thwart them.

So far the media had not made that connection, so no great outcry was raised. But it was more urgent than ever that they find and stop Karl Neff—and whoever was behind him.

Stone asked, "Who do you think is behind him?"

"We don't know. But someone is supplying him with money and equipment. Maybe there are answers at the Club Heppe."

Hog said, "We don't speaka da lingo."

"Loughlin does. You go with him as bodyguards. Let him do all the talking."

Loughlin asked, "What's my cover?"

"You could be a high-class pimp," Hog suggested.

Stone said, "He's an international arms dealer. That way somebody'll listen. It might give us a chance to get into the back room."

"Very good," Carol agreed. "But what if you run into Neff? He's seen you."

"We'll cross that bridge when we get to it," Stone said. "No one else has seen us, except the woman, Eva Ullman. Let's go there tonight—keep the pressure up."

Neff was disgusted. He met with two of the men who had gone to Trummer Road expecting to corral one or all of the Americans. "You botched the job!" he shouted at them.

"These are not ordinary men," one said. He was Georg Werfel.

"They die when you put a bullet through them!" Neff snapped.

"But that is not easy to do." Werfel shrugged. "We simply underestimated them. We were too sure the woman, Ullman, would be believed."

The second man, Uto Schrenck, said, "It was the rendezvous itself that alerted them."

"Perhaps," Neff admitted grudgingly. "But they have killed too many of us. Deal with them at once." He snapped his fingers. "They must not interrupt everything we have planned."

"We have free rein?"

"Yes, yes, of course. Just do it. The situation, as it is, is intolerable."

"What about Eva?" Georg asked.

"I have not yet decided what will be done about her." Neff waved his hand. "You have a job to do. I suggest you get about it." He turned on his heel.


The Club Heppe was off the beaten tourist track in a less than desirable section, on a street of drab and occasionally garish fronts. Heppe had a small tan-and-black sign on the street and an arrow pointing down a flight of steps.

As they paused in the doorway, they could hear raucous music coming from below; someone was shouting a song. They were dressed in jeans and checked shirts, Hog with a wide-brimmed hat, Stone with a knitted cap. Loughlin, as befit his more exalted station, was better dressed—his big frame in a suit that was slightly baggy to hide the automatic pistol at the small of his back.

Near the bottom of the steps was a landing where a bearded man sat behind a card table holding a number of boxes. He wore a red headband and greeted them in German.

Loughlin replied politely and bought three tickets. He led down the last half dozen steps to the floor, where a fat *fräulein* took the tickets and yelled at them to find seats. It was necessary to yell because at the bottom of the steps the noise level was horrendous. A band was playing at the far end of the room, a girl was screeching into a microphone, and everyone in the room was apparently talking at once.

There was a bar to the right and Loughlin headed for it, pushing his way through the crowd. Hog had been severely warned beforehand to keep his mouth shut. His Texas twang would stand out and possibly brand them all as interlopers . . . there being no tourists in the throng. So Hog merely grunted as he followed the Brit.

Loughlin found a tiny spot at the bar and shoved into it, ordering beer for himself and his friends. When the steins came, Loughlin loudly asked the bartender if Ignaz had been in the bar tonight. Before the man could reply, Loughlin said he had a shipment of AK-47s for him and was worried about payment.

The barman said he didn't know an Ignaz, and went on with his work. Loughlin said he thought everyone knew Ignaz.

Grumbling, he turned away and they found a table, a postage-stamp-sized round table on which they placed the drinks. They sat down, rubbing shoulders with those around them. A man leaned over and spoke to Stone, who smiled and nodded.

Loughlin shook his head and growled at the man, who moved away quickly. "Gay," Loughlin said. Hog chuckled.

The girl at the microphone was replaced by a young man with leather lungs who barked several songs and capered with the musicians. Then a nearly naked trio appeared and gyrated to howls and whistles, and as their number ended, the girls pulled off bras and shook their red nipples. Hog hooted and had to be poked to prevent him from inviting them to the table.

As the musicians settled into another number a waiter passed by their table and dropped an envelope in front of Loughlin. The man was gone before Loughlin could grab him.

Hog said softly, "Another girl wants his body."

Loughlin opened the envelope. "It's a man's name and number."

Stone took the proffered slip of paper. Under the name and telephone number was the single word: *Guns*. He smiled.

"Hooked one," Loughlin said.

"Let's get outa here," Stone said. He rose and the others followed. Hog brought up the rear, pushing through the crowd. With the door in sight, someone turned in front of Hog and an elbow struck his chin.

"Son of a bitch!" Hog said aloud.

The man who had struck him halted. *"Amerikaner!"* He swore in German and spit at Hog. Hog's fist knocked him sprawling. But others took up the yell, *"Amerikaner! Amerikaner!"* They surged around the three.

"My word," Loughlin said. "You fellows are unpopular." He hit the nearest man a crushing blow. Hog picked up a man in a T-shirt and threw him at the mob.

Then Stone got the door open to the stairs—someone had shut it, apparently trying to keep the three in. He tossed a chair at the nearest men in the crowd and backed up the steps.

Hog tackled the man with the headband and tossed him down the stairs and they went out into the night.


"You told me you'd gotten rid of her!" Britt shouted. "Why is she still around?"

"I'm not seeing her," Neff growled. "If she's around it's not my doing. It's all over between us."

Britt glared at him. "You could send her away if you wanted to. Why don't you?"

"She's a free person, for God's sake! Stop pounding on me! She means nothing at all to me. Why can't you get it through your head?"

"She was with you the other night."

"Which night?"

Britt lit a cigarette and blew smoke at him. "At the factory. Uto told me she was there."

"Yes, she was there. All I did was get her out of the place before the police caught her. She could tell them too much. Be reasonable—what else could I do? And she recognized one of the men who raided us."

"I didn't know that. . . ."

"He was a man she knew in Britian. It may give us a line on them."

Britt studied him. "Where is she now?"

"I had Georg take her to the estate."

"You said it yourself—she knows too much. She has to go."

Neff sneered. "Are you making the decisions for us now? I didn't realize you had become the leader."

She stubbed out the cigarette with hard, quick movements. "All right. Let's not fight. But you know how I feel about her."

"I know. But try not to show it in front of the others. Eva is important to us for the moment, till we find out what she knows about the man she called Terry."

"Yes, Karl . . ."

# Chapter Eight

The telephone number Loughlin had received in the note from "Eva" had been traced by the Communications Section and found to be a dead end.

It was a wall phone in an area where perhaps a thousand people had access. They had only one other lead: the Club Heppe note about the guns. In the Operations building, with the Communications Section men monitoring the call, Loughlin dialed the number on the slip of paper.

It rang three times and a voice said, "Yes?" It was a sharp, incisive voice and for a moment Loughlin could not tell its gender. He said, "You gave me a note about guns at the Heppe?"

"No. I did not. This is an apartment house. What name do you want?"

"Sorry," Loughlin said, and hung up.

It proved to be an apartment building, the Communications men said when they ran down the number.

Stone said, "Maybe someone got cold feet at the last minute."

"And maybe we oughta go back to that there club," Hog offered. "See who runs the joint."

Stone nodded. "Good idea. Maybe it belongs to Neff. But it would be handy to know the room setup. We might break into the john instead of the office."

• • •

Walter Kolpe worked at the Operations building as a janitor. He was sixty-one, stooped and wrinkled, and lived with his wife in a row house a mile from the job.

Johann Dicot had him tailed for a week and found that Kolpe went often, after work, to a small liquor shop near his apartment. He himself went there and struck up a conversation with Kolpe, bought him a drink and met him again the next day. He asked Kolpe's advice. Should his young nephew apply for a job at the Operations building? What was necessary?

It was necessary to speak English well enough to get along. And one had to undergo a security check. . . . No, he never handled anything that was classified, but the check was required just the same. And yes, he knew the building very well, having cleaned it, with others, for two years.

Dicot asked, "Could you draw me a plan of it?"

Kolpe was startled. "Why do you want such a thing?"

Dicot laid a packet of money on the table between them, concealing it from the others in the shop with his body. "I want it."

Walter Kolpe eyed the money and bit his lip.

"Just a plan, showing the rooms and what's in them. And this is yours." He touched the packet with a finger. "Count it if you like."

With trembling hands, Kolpe riffled the packet and put it down. Never in his life had he had so much money in his hands at one time. He took a long breath. Just a plan? What harm would that do?

He nodded. "When do you want it?"

"As soon as possible."

It took Walter two days to draw the plans of the three floors. And when he brought the sheets of paper to Dicot, meeting him in secret, Dicot went over them in minute detail, all his attention centered on the rooms where the three American civilians were quartered.

They were on the third floor, the last three rooms on the south side of the building, overlooking a commercial building.

"What kind of a building?" Dicot asked.

"It's a warehouse."

"Each of the rooms where the Americans are quartered has two windows overlooking the warehouse?" Dicot bent over the paper. "Six windows in all?"

"Yes."

Dicot gave Kolpe the money, warning him to say nothing about the plan he'd drawn. "No matter how much they question you."

"Why would they question me?"

"Say nothing," Dicot warned. He showed the man out. Walter went home with grave misgivings. The money in his pocket felt very comforting, but his conscience began to bother him so that he was irritable and defensive. He had not told his wife about the meetings or the packet of money—he was afraid to tell her—and so he could not spend it. He hid it away and went about like a man with ten minutes to live. He could not use the money and he could not give it up.

Johann Dicot took the plans to Karl Neff, explaining how he'd obtained them. They laid the third-floor plan on a table. Kolpe had marked everything in his neat penciled printing. The names of the three Americans were lettered precisely. "Stone, Loughlin, Wiley," each in the space that was his room.

"Stone is the leader," Dicot said, "according to the old man. If we remove him it should take the heart out of the others."

Neff nodded, studying the plan. "It will probably be impossible to kill all of them at once. Are you certain you can get into the warehouse?"

"Yes, certain. Georg investigated it today. There are two night watchmen, both older men. We will have no trouble with them." He snapped his fingers.

"But you will get only once chance." Neff looked at the other. "Is it a difficult shot?"

"Not for an expert. We've got three Heckler and Koch G3s. They fire five hundred and fifty rounds per minute. One magazine ought to do it."

"Twenty rounds?"

Dicot grinned. "We'll tear the wall off."

Neff nodded. "All right. Do it."

Walter Kolpe's attitude changed completely after his last visit with Dicot. The money was in a safe place but his conscience was not. And his attitude change was noted by half a dozen people in the Operations building. They were, after all, persons directly connected with espionage and covert situations. They could recognize the signs—and they reported them.

Kolpe was immediately taken aside and interrogated.

Dicot selected Conrad Oelze as the sniper. Oelze had been twelve years in the army and was an expert with all types of weapons. He was given the G3 and a place to practice. He was promised money and a couple of girls for a week.

The warehouse was a huge, dark pile, gray and silent when Johann Dicot cut a chain holding closed the gate of a chain-link fence. Georg Werfel and Uto Schrenck entered the yard and tied up the two watchmen and put them in an office. Conrad Oelze, with the assault rifle in a plastic-wrapped package, came in after them, guided by Dicot. They walked up a long ramp and Dicot crowbarred a door open. They went up a huge elevator to the third floor, getting out on a dusty landing. There were twenty-foot-high stacks of crates and boxes all about.

With a pencil flash, Dicot led the way through them to one side of the warehouse. "Here we are," he said. He clicked off the flash and pulled aside a piece of dark canvas covering a window, and Oelze saw the Operations building, only a short distance away.

Dicot pointed. "Those windows on the right. That's where they are. The last two are Stone's."

Oelze studied them. Blank rectangles, no lights on inside. About eighty feet away, an easy shot. He'd had many worse assignments. He looked at the plan. The old man had even drawn in the positions of the beds. The old bugger had been efficient.

He looked to the left and right. the next building to the

left was too far away, but to the right was another warehouse and a tower sticking up close by. No one would be able to tell where the shots had come from—not for a while. Getting out after the shooting would be no problem.

There would be lots of sound because he would tear the building over there to shreds. Oelze smiled. He was going to enjoy this.

They borrowed the old red fiat from the motor pool again and drove to the Club Heppe after midnight. They left the car a block away and prowled by the entrance, trying to look as if they belonged. Loughlin paused by the door; there was music coming up from below, a few shouts. Did the place never close?

None of them had seen anything that looked like offices off the barroom when they'd been there before. Probably the offices were above, on the ground floor. There was a street door without a nameplate, but it was sturdy and had two locks. Very impressive.

On the next street over was a short alley between two apartment buildings; it approached the back of the club building and was choked with barrels, boxes and other trash and ended at a high board fence.

With Hog breaking a path, they climbed over the debris and slid over the fence. There was very little room between the fence and the club building, which was brick, painted or whitewashed. There were two rows of barred windows and a small door. Above the barred windows were two more small windows, unbarred.

"Piece of cake," Loughlin said. He went up the side of the building, using the bars as hand- and footholds, and put his elbow through the glass of one window, reached in and opened it. He grinned at them and went in, to pop his head out in a moment.

"Come on up."

They climbed up and joined him in a small room. A pencil flash revealed dusty boxes and stacked papers, a few file cabinets and nothing else.

Stone opened a door that gave onto a hallway; there were other doors, the floor was dark. Nothing but empty rooms that smelled stale. Two contained unmade beds.

They went downstairs to the second floor. Here were four offices, one very large and comfortable looking. It contained easy chairs, a television set and a bar. In one corner was a copying machine. Using the pencil flash they searched the desk and made copies of a few papers that looked suspicious. It was enormously handy to have the machine.

"We ought to leave a thank-you note," Loughlin said.

Hog and Stone rifled the other offices, pocketing small items of value and money to make it look like a sneak thief had been there. Then they went out the same way they'd entered, and walked to the car.

When they returned to the Operations building they laid out the stolen papers on a table and examined them under proper lights, with Carol and Meydel helping. Nothing much. There were several references to something called Reinsburg. . . .

None of the papers showed ownership of the club and they could find no reference to Karl Neff. However, one name did turn up twice: Rudolf von Schiller.

"Von Schiller is dead," Meydel said with some surprise. "He was a Nazi during the war and died when the Russians entered Berlin."

"Maybe this is his son."

"Maybe. I did not know he had children." Meydel shrugged. "We will run a check on him."

Carol frowned. "There has been an interesting development tonight. We interrogated an employee of the building, a man named Walter Kolpe. He was employed as a janitor. He was thought to be acting curiously, but when we began to question him, he became very unstrung and we had to call in a doctor. Kolpe had a heart attack in the interrogation room and is now in the infirmary, unable to speak."

"It sounds like fear," Stone said.

Carol nodded. "We think so too. He's hiding something. He had no access to classified information so he could not have sold anything of value."

Meydel said, "He might have sold information about some *person* here."

"Such as us." Loughlin made a face. "But we do not come and go on any schedule."

"We've used that little Fiat twice," Hog remarked. "Better not do it no more."

"Good show," Loughlin agreed.

"We'll keep you informed on his progress—just in case," Carol said.

"What about his wife?" Stone asked. "Does she know anything?"

"No, apparently not. Whatever Kolpe did he kept to himself."

"And he did *something*," Meydel said, "to get him into this state. We are sure it concerned this facility. Kolpe had no problems, according to his wife. They had two children, long since grown. No particular problems with them."

Stone said, "I'd like to know more about this von Schiller. How sure are you that he died?"

Meydel shrugged elaborately. "You know how records were in those days. A great many Nazis escaped to other countries, . . ."

"I see. So the information about his death is suspect."

"I'm afraid it is. We have several photographs of him, but of course they are forty years old. However, I will get you his file." Meydel made a note.

"Thanks."

They went upstairs to bed. It was late. Stone did not bother to open the drapes to pull up a window. He doffed his clothes and fell into bed . . . asleep in moments after his head touched the pillow.

# Chapter Nine

Walter Kolpe had a good night. He was stabilizing, the doctors said; they thought he would be able to talk soon. His wife sat in the waiting room, knitting for hours, talking to the nurses when they stopped by her. . . .

Carol Jenner got hourly reports on his condition, and just after noon of the first day after his attack, she was summoned to his room. The doctor was there in his white coat, teetering on his heels.

"You have two minutes with him, *fräulein*."

Kolpe looked terrible, she thought. He lay in a jungle of tubes and equipment, his watery eyes blinking as she spoke to him softly.

"Walter, what brought you here?"

"P-plans," he said. "I drew plans."

"Plans of what—of this building?"

He tried to nod. *"Ja, ja . . ."*

The doctor pushed her aside. "One moment."

She retreated to the foot of the bed. Plans of the building?! Apparently he had sold plans of the building to someone. She thought immediately of the three men. But their quarters were on the third floor. No one could get into the building and up to that floor without— She bit her lip. The rooms had windows!

Carol ran out and rushed to the stairs. The infirmary was on the second floor. She climbed to the third and ran down the hallway to pound on Stone's door.

He said, "Come in. . . ."

She opened the door. He was sitting on the floor with Hog. They were busy cleaning weapons and looked at her with surprise. Stone asked, "What is it?"

Carol took a long breath, glancing at the draped windows. "Walter Kolpe." She sank into a chair. "He said he sold plans of this building to someone."

"Well, damn him!" Hog said.

Stone looked at the windows immediately. Hog followed the glance. "You figger they got us zeroed in?"

Stone asked, "What else did Kolpe say?"

"Nothing. The doctor chased me out. He may not know who he sold them to, of course, but we'll question him more when the doctor allows it."

Stone nodded, his gaze returning to the windows. "Tex is right. They've got us zeroed in. What's out there?"

"Warehouses," she said. "Two or three of them, and a tower."

"They couldn't figger to git all of us," Hog remarked. "They'd be lucky as hell t' git one."

"They're desperate?" Carol bit her lower lip.

"Maybe revenge," Hog said, grinning. "We done 'em a little dirt." He clicked a magazine into place and slipped the Walther into a holster. "We goin' after them, boss man?"

"Let the army do it," Carol said.

Stone shook his head. "They're getting personal. We'll do this job ourselves."

She rolled her eyes. "I'm going to have another conference with Captain Brockhof. I can see it coming."

In Hog's room, with the room dark, they opened the draperies and, using night glasses, scanned the warehouses opposite, in the hope of spotting something to give them a clue. Stone paid special attention to the nearest warehouse. There were windows that faced theirs; a sniper would want the best shot he could get. . . .

An hour's watching turned up nothing.

Then Loughlin suggested they turn the lights on in

Stone's room. "One of us could walk through—tease 'em a little."

"Good idea," Stone agreed. He and Hog watched through the glasses as Loughlin went into Stone's room.

In a moment Hog said, "I see something . . . second window from the end. Now it's gone."

"That's good enough." Stone put the glasses down. "Let's get at it."

They went downstairs and out to the street. It was late and misty out; it had rained slightly early in the evening and the streets were still damp. The air felt balmy as they walked to the warehouse.

The warehouse was huge, dark and silent. If snipers were using it they had either eliminated the night watchmen or bribed them. Stone thought it likely they had forced their way in. Neff's group was not known for negotiation.

How many terrorists were in the building? Probably not many. They would need only one to do the shooting. More would only get in the way when they beat their retreat.

There was a chain-link fence at the front with a heavy gate. The gate was held closed by a sturdy chain and a padlock.

The chain had been cut . . . and the links positioned so the gate looked to be locked. Hog opened the gate silently and they went through and refastened the chain.

There was a long ramp up to a door, which was ajar.

Loughlin said, "They plan to do this job tonight."

Stone nodded. "They've got the positions of our beds. Any heavy weapon would tear off the wall of the Operations building like cheese."

"A man ain't safe in his own goddamn bed," Hog complained.

Inside the door it was dark. Stone said, "Look for stairs." He had a pencil flash and used it sparingly. They were surrounded by crates and machinery; the room had a curious smell to it.

"Over here," Loughlin said softly.

There were steps against the far wall, with a pipe banister. Stone went up first, feeling his way, the Uzi ready. The second floor was packed solid with cardboard boxes, only narrow paths between them.

The steps continued up along the wall and Stone moved slowly, not daring to use the flash. It was pitch black and he felt each step before he put his foot on it. Hog was behind him, a hand on his belt.

He stopped, hearing voices. Ahead of them somewhere a man was speaking; he could smell tobacco. So, two of them at least.

There were two more steps, then the top, and it was slightly lighter. He could see the stacks of crates all about them. The sounds came from a short distance. Two men were talking in normal voices, no need to modulate them. . . .

There were several paths through the stacks—which one should they take? Stone wished he could use the flash. It was annoying having to go blind, not knowing what they were up against . . . not knowing how to get to the bad guys. He swore under his breath.

Loughlin pointed to one path, then to himself. Then he pointed to another and to Hog, suggesting they divide.

Stone shook his head. It might be fatal to divide in an unknown situation.

He was about to move forward when the night came apart.

Very close by, someone was firing at the Operations building, automatic fire that sounded like heavy artillery in the confined space. Stone heard the sniper change magazines and fire again. He rushed forward with Hog and Loughlin at his heels.

They came out far to the right of the shooter. Rounding a stack they saw him stand up and slap another magazine into the rifle. As he did so, he saw them.

Stone saw the man's face change—the light was poor —the man yelled something and swung the gun around. Stone fired the Uzi, seeing him crumple.

A second man fired at them and ran to his right.

Stone heard Loughlin say: "Shit!" Then he rushed after the fleeing man—and halted in the blackness. The son of a bitch knew the place and he did not. He could hear footsteps fading out, then silence.

He went back to the body. The sniper had been hit half a dozen times and was a bloody mop, sprawling on the floor. Loughlin was holding his arm, blood leaking through his fingers.

"Are you hit?"

"It grazed me," the Brit said. "Just a scratch. Did the other one get away?"

"I'm afraid so." Stone ripped the shirt off the dead man and tore a clean piece and bound up Loughlin's wound. "That'll hold it till we get back."

Loughlin said, "Why don't I go back and get the cops up here. Maybe somebody can identify this guy."

"Good idea. And you can stop off at the infirmary."

Hog had been gazing through the night glasses the sniper had used. "Our rooms are cut to shit, neighbors. This guy used a G3 on 'em."

Stone took the binoculars. The wall of the building looked like cheesecloth. All six windows had been blasted out.

Hog said, "You figger somebody's mad at us?"

Loughlin laughed and walked back to the stairs using the flashlight.

Alois Stoltz debated with himself for a day or two, then went to his captain to tell the story his sister had told him. There was no proof, he said, but his sister was not an imaginative woman; there must be something behind it all.

"What is the man's name?" the police captain asked.

"Danzig. It's all I know."

"What does he look like?"

Alois described the man he'd met once.

"And what did he do for a living?"

Alois shook his head. "I don't know, sir. My sister says he had money at odd times and told her various stories about how he got it."

"You met him once? Did he seem to you the kind of man who could shoot Gerd Helbing?"

Alois shook his head again. "I just don't know, sir. He

was a strange one. How is one to know by looking?"

"Hmmm. Yes." The captain thought for a moment. "Well, we will put out a bulletin and bring him in for questioning. Thank you, Stoltz."

Stoltz nodded and went out.

Eva Ullman was thirty-eight, a very good-looking woman. Not beautiful, for beauty would be a liability in her chosen profession; she was what some would call handsome. She was careful not to use cosmetics as some did; she did not want to be remembered.

But it was time for her to get out... out of Germany and out of the service. Life was passing her by; it wasn't the same for a man, or at least she felt it was not. Seeing Terry Loughlin had been a terrible jolt, and an astonishment.

However, there was a more pressing reason for her to leave Germany behind. Karl Neff was wise to her, she was sure of it. Was she slated to be killed?

Despite all her training and experience she could feel ice along her spine. He was ruthless.

That one word had been surprised out of her: "Terry." She had uttered it in Karl's presence... and regretted it every moment since. So far he had not questioned her. When they left the warehouse that night he had put her into a car and she'd been driven to Reinsburg at once. She had not seen him since.

They told her, when she insisted on an answer, that he was busy in Frankfurt.

And now she feared his return.

Reinsburg was a very old mansion. The estate belonged to a shadowy figure—no one would tell her who. It was used by Neff and several others in like organizations—terrorists. Who would look for a terrorist group in a fine old and sedate setting like Reinsburg?

Potato Face was here, too. She thought of Danzig that way. He followed her about though she did everything she could to rid herself of him. He was a disgusting little man, with the morals of a pig. He was here until the heat cooled, as the Americans said. He was implicated in something, she did not know what. Probably a killing. Neff's group was good at that.

Could she get away from Reinsburg and not be caught? It might be done if she were an eighteen-year-old man, strong as an oak and quick, able to run miles at top speed. Unfortunately the estate was far out in the country, with only two roads leading past it. The railroad was miles away—too far to reach. She was in good physical condition, but she doubted if she could evade the all-out search that would be made for her if she took off.

No one made her stand assembly, but she knew they kept track of her movements. If she went anywhere at all on the estate she was sure to see one of the "servants" watching her. The servants were all Neff's men...and women. She had no access to cars or horses without one of them along.

It was some small consolation that she knew they watched Potato Face too. Karl trusted no one.

And she was aware that Britt Gericke hated her.

Her job had demanded a close relationship with Neff for a time, and it had led to being his lover. Neff was not a good lover and she had had to work very hard at it to keep him interested. He thought of nothing but his work—and his plans. And of course the relationship had faltered and finally ground to a halt. He had moved her out and, in a while, had moved Britt in.

Eva often wondered how Britt could stand the man, but evidently she could. Perhaps she was made of the same hard material. Except that Britt was the jealous type.

Would Britt influence him to have her, Eva, killed?

# Chapter Ten

Rudolf von Schiller had been one of the most powerful men in Nazi Germany. He had Hitler's ear—and everyone knew it; this alone increased his power tremendously. And von Schiller loved power.

When the Third Reich collapsed under the hammering of the Allied armies, von Schiller went into hiding and became very irrational and despondent, thinking of suicide. But loyal and devoted aides smuggled him out of the country and took him to Africa, where he lived for several years under a French name, far from traveled routes.

There he regained his sanity and began to make plans for the return of the party. With excellently forged documents he made many trips to Germany, gathering in strings, meeting with old comrades who thought as he did, and making more plans.

But politics had changed since the war, and von Schiller realized that the old Germany could never be again. But there were new routes to power. And one of them was through terrorism.

The idea of terrorism was not new to von Schiller. Had not the SS engaged in terrorism throughout the war? Himmler had been an expert at it. The young zealots could learn from him, especially in the matter of torture.

The younger generations had other things to learn as well, von Schiller thought. He and his close-knit group had been past masters at looting. They squirreled away millions, obscuring their tracks so the Allied investigators had never uncovered a centime. This was the vast wealth von Schiller was using to make his way back into power.

Neff was his mailed fist in Frankfurt, centering his operations at Reinsburg. Von Schiller came there occasionally for staff meetings. At one of these, the following day, he learned about the three Americans who had done them so much damage.

"Three men are too much for you?"

"They have been amazingly lucky," Neff replied. "Luck runs that way sometimes."

Von Schiller did not pursue the subject. But when he left the meeting he talked with an aide, giving him certain instructions. That done, he forgot the entire matter; there were many other pressing demands on his time. Three annoying pests were nothings in the larger scheme of things.

The aide, Carlo Vanner, returned to Neff. "What can you tell me of the three Americans?"

"Why do you ask?" said Neff. "Is von Schiller going after them himself?"

"He has referred the matter to me."

"I see. Then he is displeased with me?"

Vanner shrugged. "Do not read mysterious things into what von Schiller does. He is a direct man, after all. Tell me about the Americans."

Neff shook his head. "I have seen only one of them, briefly. You had better talk to Johann."

"Very well."

Johann Dicot was cautious with Vanner, knowing who he was. Vanner was one of von Schiller's right-hand men. He said, "We know the three Americans work for a clandestine section of the U.S. government. We also know they were in Vietnam and other places. Thus they all have great experience in remaining in one piece. They are obviously expert with all weapons, can see in the dark and have outguessed us so far."

"You sound as if it is an unequal battle."

"I have vast respect for men who have beaten me the way they have. If one makes the slightest mistake with them—he is dead."

"They cannot see into your brain," Vanner said with an edge to his voice. "It is possible to make plans they can know nothing about."

"But carrying them through is another matter."

"You say they have outguessed you. Is it possible they have an informer in your ranks?"

Dicot shook his head. "I don't see how. Our people have been checked and checked again. Karl said the Americans are lucky. I agree. They have been."

"I don't believe in luck. Where do the Americans stay?"

"They have quarters in the Operations building, but we do not know where . . . since we destroyed their quarters recently."

Vanner nodded. "What further plans have you discussed concerning the Americans?"

Dicot smiled. "None at the moment." He did not mention the woman, Eva Ullman. If this so-important aide to von Schiller was so damned smart, let him find his own information.

Vanner thanked him and turned away. He went outside to the automobile park and went at once to the Club Heppe. He was mildly surprised to find that it had been burgled. Nothing but small items had been taken, according to the manager, Fritz Auer. The thieves had broken a window to get in.

"Let me see the window," Vanner said. It was on the third floor. He looked out the window to the ground. Someone had had to climb the side of the building to get to it. Would a sneak thief, after a few coins, go to that effort?

Auer was certain the three Americans had been in his club, and had started a fight there. At least, a fight had started while they were there. Vanner questioned a bartender about it. One of the Americans spoke perfect German, the man said. He had asked about someone in the bar—

"What name?" Vanner demanded.

"I don't remember the name. He said he was to deliver guns to this person. It was shortly after that the fight started."

And shortly after that, Vanner mused, the club was broken into. Maybe it had been a fishing expedition—the Americans were hoping to find something. It was the best he could come up with.

Auer provided him a sleeping room and the next morning he drove by the American Operations building on a motorcycle, just to look it over. It was a well-built structure. And he could depend on it—the place was well guarded, though he saw no obvious guards.

Could he get someone inside to inform him of the Americans' movements? It would be an enormous advantage. Of course it would be an unusual person—he or she would have to pass a difficult security examination. . . . He could think of no one at the moment. Perhaps von Schiller would know someone.

As it stood, he would be always a step or two behind the three Americans. He would have to react to their actions. It was hard to make plans when there was no way of knowing what the enemy would do next. It was imperative that he know what they would do next.

At the same time he knew that any new employee in the building would be watched, and that person would never get close to the Americans. Could he bribe someone who already was?

Neff's men had bribed a janitor and it had worked against them. Apparently the janitor had informed his employers. At any rate the plan had gone kaput. He must think about this. . . .

Hans Meydel had looked into the matter of Reinsburg. "I decided it must be a place," he told them. "To try to track down every person of that name would take many years. But there are two small towns named Reinsburg. Unfortunately, they are both some distance from Frankfurt. Is that important?"

"It could be," Stone said. "Could it be the name of a house, like in England?"

"That is my next project."

Loughlin remarked, "It could be the name of a club . . . or a business."

Meydel sighed. "Yes. And it might not be a place at

all." He shrugged. "It could be a code name."

"If it is," Hog said, "we's out of grits."

Meydel stared at him. "Grits?"

"It's a delicacy," Stone said, "in some parts of the U.S."

"Ahhhh."

The dead man in the warehouse had been identified as Conrad Oelze; his fingerprints were on file. He had not been known to be a part of any terrorist organization—but then, they did not know all the names. Oelze had no immediate family. No relative came forward when his picture was printed in the daily papers. It was given out that he had been the victim of an accident.

As Carol Jenner had expected, Captain Brockhof interviewed her and others at some length and learned very little. Brockhof went away, very annoyed at diplomatic immunity. Dead bodies kept turning up and he could make no arrests.

Aside from the mystery of Reinsburg, there were no leads to Karl Neff. Paid informers were sent to every part of Frankfurt, listening, asking questions, snooping—but nothing pertinent turned up. Neff had apparently stepped off the planet for a time. Nothing further was heard from Eva Ullman. Loughlin thought it felt like the lull before the storm.

The three were given other quarters in the center of the building, without windows. The entire building was shuffled, making the plan Walter Kolpe had drawn useless to their enemies. Everything was changed. New doors were cut and several secret entrances made.

When they went out at night to watch the Club Heppe, Stone and the others used one of the new exits.


Carol Vanner had installed watchers about the Operations building, keeping all sides of it under surveillance around the clock. And thus he discovered the secret entrances not long after they were put into use.

He kept in touch with his watchers by radio, and when one reported that three men answering the descriptions of the Americans had just left the building, Vanner swung into action.

He had a squad of trained men, twelve in number, heavily armed, and he sent them after the three. "None of them
is to survive," he ordered. "Bring me the bodies."

The Americans were in a small DKW and were immediately aware that they were being followed. Driving, Stone
headed at once into a series of narrow streets, where it was
impossible for the pursuers to come alongside. The leader
of the pursuers was Augie Appel. He had split his men into
two groups and tried to radio ahead to intercept the Americans, but he found that was impossible too.

He nearly lost the Americans in the maze of narrow
streets, but his second group found them again and a lucky
burst of fire mauled the small car's engine. The Americans
piled out and scattered.

At Stone's command, they were out of the stalled car
in seconds. Hog jumped for the nearest doorway on the
right and dropped to one knee, whirling and firing a burst
at the black car that sped by him. A row of bullets stitched
across the door just above his head. He fired another burst;
the right rear tire exploded. The car veered left and
smashed into a storefront.

Hog glanced along the street. If he ran to the left it
would be into a lighted area and they would cut him down.
He rose and rammed his elbow into the door and a panel
gave. He pushed it in and reached in to unlock the door.

He was in a hallway that smelled dusty. Stairs led up to
two more doors. He paused to look along the street. Stone
and Loughlin had gone to their left and had probably run
between the buildings—he could just make out an alleyway there.

Five men were running toward him from the smashed
car. Hog gave them a quick burst and ran up the stairs.
Both doors were locked. He kicked one in and entered, the
Uzi ready. He was in a storeroom.

It was a long narrow room. He could barely see in the
dim light from a row of undraped windows. He slammed
the door shut and shoved half a dozen heavy boxes in front
of it. That would buy him a minute or two.

Running down the room, he stopped at the last window

and pushed it open. Someone pounded on the door. Smiling, Hog turned and fired five aimed shots at it. The pounding stopped.

He looked out. He was about twenty feet from the ground, a dark mass. He could not tell what was beneath him. Above was the roof, only two feet away. He slung the Uzi over his shoulder and swung out, grasping the metal frame of the window, reaching for the eave. There was a storm drain that seemed solid. He grabbed it and pulled himself up, sliding onto the roof, panting.

From the sounds below him they had pushed their way into the room. Someone shouted commands in German.

It was a mostly flat roof, with pipes sticking up, a few wires and some sort of a boxlike structure at the far end. Hog ran lightly to that end and jumped to the next roof; it sloped gently up and was lighted by a sign to his right.

Shots screamed by his ear as he jumped and fell flat, searching for where they'd come from. Probably from the street. He scurried away from the street side, hearing yells from below. They had him pinpointed—they thought. Men had climbed onto the roof behind him, the same place he'd climbed up. Several had powerful flashlights. When they turned them his way, Hog ducked behind a chimney.

He ought to get the hell off this roof.

Three men were on the roof behind him, coming fast, bent over. Hog waited till the first man jumped, then fired a burst that caught his pursuer in midair. The body convulsed and fell between the buildings. His second burst threw a running man back to sprawl motionless. The third man ducked flat, firing wildly.

Hog retreated, keeping the chimney between him and the other. At the roof's end, he looked down on a lower building. In a moment he had let himself down and looked into the street.

Someone was shouting something that sounded like "Polizei," and in another moment he heard the sound of sirens. He walked to the back of the building and climbed down into a garden.

He had hardly raised a sweat.

# Chapter Eleven

Augie Appel had lost two men, a third wounded, in the encounter with the big American on the roofs. They had lost him and had to disperse when the police approached.

"The man was a tiger!" he said to Carlo Vanner. "He never missed, and the light was bad for shooting. Are the others like this one?"

"He was lucky," Vanner growled, repeating what Karl Neff had said, but as he uttered the words he knew it was not luck. They were up against very unusual opponents. These three men obviously had vast experience in firefights, could not be surprised into stupid mistakes, and would chew up and spit out anyone sent against them. Unless that someone was an expert.

Hans Meydel, working with an old map of Frankfurt, made a discovery. During the time of Bismarck, a vast estate outside of Frankfurt had been called Reinsburg, after its owner and builder, Count Reinsburg. Now the estate was much smaller; tracts had been sold off over the years. It was now listed as Soldan, and so marked on all modern maps.

"Neff's group may be using the old name," he said to Stone. "There are some pictures of the place, but they are very old and possibly of no value."

"Can you get some aerial photographs?"

Meydel smiled. "We can have surveillance helicopters fly over it and take pictures."

"Very good. That's the ticket."

The German looked at him. "Ticket?"

"Just an expression."

"Ah."

The chopper pilot was ordered to make one single flyover at fifteen hundred feet and return to base. The photographer would have one chance to take his pictures—so that those on the ground would not become suspicious.

This was done the next morning, an hour before midday, and the resulting pictures were rushed to Carol Jenner's desk. She tacked them up on the walls and studied them.

There was a main house, very large and old, with extensive gardens and a circular drive in front. There was a row of garages to one side, with a courtyard; three automobiles were visible, one a dark blue VW beetle.

Behind the house was a landing strip, a tall pole with a sock, and a wide, low building that was probably a small hangar, though no plane was visible. There was a greenhouse, and several small shedlike buildings and fields. Most of the estate was open fields and forest.

"Where do they get their money?" Loughlin asked. "Can we find out who owns this layout?"

"We'll try," Carol said. "It may be a legal tangle."

"Someone must pay the taxes."

"Okay," Stone said. "Now we know where they are."

"Send in the marines!" Hog remarked.

Stone shook his head. "We need some of them alive. One leads us to the next, and so on. Our job is to bring in Neff. He may be here," he said, tapping one of the photos, "and he may not be." He glanced at Loughlin. "Your friend Eva may be there, too."

"I had thought of that."

Hog frowned. "Then we'd better look over the lay of the ground. They maybe got land mines and booby traps all over the goddamn place."

They took the photos back to their quarters and sat around with cigarettes and beer, discussing the problem.

They were probably watched—they had to assume that. So they'd have to leave the building by secret means. The simplest way would be to conceal themselves in one or another of the supply trucks that came into the motor area each week to unload.

"Won't they suspect that?" Loughlin asked.

"Suspecting and knowing are different things," Stone said. "If we each go in a different truck and are clever about ducking out of it, we should be home free. Then we'd rendezvous somewhere."

"There's a better way," Hog said.

They looked at him.

He grinned. "We used a chopper to take the pictures, huh? So it lands on the roof and we get in. Are they goin' to follow a chopper across town?"

Stone laughed. He got up and went to the door. "I'll get it squared away."

Just after dusk the three took off in a Huey chopper and made a wide sweep over the city toward the north. Reinsburg was almost due south of the city, and it was an hour before they approached it, flying just above treetops and landing in a tiny clearing. They were, the pilot said, about a mile from the main building. He wished them luck and took off.

They were in a pine forest in rolling country. They wore combat fatigues and carried tiny radios to communicate with each other, should they become separated.

There was no way to know if they were on Reinsburg estate property or not. Perhaps there was a fence—and if so, it might be patrolled. Moving forward in a wide line, barely in sight of each other, they came onto the fence. It was merely a marker, three strands of smooth wire with signs every hundred feet: NO TRESPASSING. There was a pathway beside the wire where four-wheeled vehicles drove; it had been used very recently.

Stone slipped easily through the wire and halted to call the others in. "This is too easy," he said. "I don't buy it that they don't have a better warning system." He peered upward at the trees around them.

Loughlin said, "I haven't spotted any wires."

Hog shook his head. "Me neither."

"It worries the hell out of me," Stone growled. "They're not simple. Let's go single file like Injuns, take it slow. You watch the trees and I'll watch the ground."

"Gotcha," Hog agreed.

They moved on, walking very slowly, Stone examining every blade of grass before taking a step.

And he found the wire.

It was dull green, very thin, only a half inch above ground, or lying on the ground. He pointed it out to them. "Let's hope this is the first one." He glanced back. "We're only a dozen yards from the fence, so it probably is. If we step on this it'll ring a bell or sound a buzzer or something—"

"An animal could step on it," Loughlin said.

"Yes. So it means there's more of these. They can plot our course by how many we step on."

Hog said, "And send a delegation to welcome us, huh?"

"Exactly. A deer would probably not move in a straight line for very long, but a man would. It will also probably tell them how many are coming."

"Dastardly," Hog said, and they both looked at him. Hog grinned. "I heard it in a James Bond movie."

"He's getting class," Loughlin remarked.

"Let's go." Stone moved out slowly again, eyes on the ground.

They found a half dozen more wires before they came to the edge of the trees and looked out across weedy fields to the houses in the near distance. There was a plane sitting at the end of the airstrip. And as they looked, a car drove out to it and a man climbed into the plane. It took off and made a graceful turn to the south and disappeared.

Were there more wires in the fields? Probably not, Stone thought. There must be miles of it in the woods; there would be another form of surveillance close to the main house, doubtless lights and maybe dogs.

The main house was in the open, some distance from the woods that crept up on three sides . . . as he recalled from the aerial photos. To get to the house they would have to cross open areas, but the moon was dark.

"There's a shed between us and the big house," Stone said, pointing. "It's not lighted on this side. We'll go across the field to it."

Hog screwed the silencer on his pistol. "And if they's dogs—the buggers'll have to go."

Stone led out in a straight line to the shed, walking at a natural pace. Anyone standing within the light on the other side could probably not see them at all.

The field was deeply furrowed and it was difficult getting across the furrows, many were weedy and some were several feet deep. The ground had probably not been used for planting for a very long time.

They reached the dark side of the low shed without incident.

On his belly, Stone looked around the end of the shed. The distance to the main house was probably eighty feet, and in between were shrubs and a low hedge that probably bordered a walk. The airstrip was off to their left, the garage area directly ahead. Several men were standing in the courtyard smoking; he could see the pinpricks of light as they sucked on cigarettes.

"No dogs," Loughlin said.

Stone shoved back. "If they had vicious dogs here, it would probably be talked about by neighbors. And that's the last thing Neff wants. He'd like to be invisible. I'm a little surprised they have so many lights on around the house."

"Because of us," Hog said, with satisfaction. "We been kickin' their ass." He patted the Uzi in his arms. "And we gonna kick it some more."

"Down low," Stone said softly. "We'll go to the corner of the big house. No shooting unless someone steps on us." He moved out, crouching low.

Hog brought up the rear, humming softly to himself.

Using the hedge for cover, they approached the main building, and Stone halted. Two men, with rifles slung over their shoulders, came walking toward them, talking German. They were on a collision course and Stone swore under his breath. There was no time to go back and nowhere to hide.

Then the two men stopped, and one put a cigarette in his mouth and the other struck a match. In that moment Hog stood up and strode to them. The two men stared at him in amazement—doubtless wondering where he had come from. One said, *"Wer ist es?"*

Then Hog grabbed each man and knocked their heads together.

It happened in seconds. The two men were on the ground, motionless, with Hog grinning at them. Loughlin said, "Jesus!"

Hog pulled off the rifles and yanked pistols from holsters. Standing, he tossed the pistols into the dark field beyond the shed. Stone and Loughlin tied the men with their own belts and Hog shoved the rifles into the shrubbery. They carried the men back to the shed and put them inside, latching the door.

The two men were probably part of a guard detail. How many others were there? Maybe they circled the house continually during their tour. If so, the two men in the shed might not be missed for a while.

Motioning, Stone led out again and this time gained the side of the house in deep shadow. The lights were all directed at the area surrounding the house, and not on it. Above their heads were windows, tightly shuttered and dark. It was a four-story house, built of gray stone, with ivy crawling the walls here and there.

Stone moved toward the back of the house; it would probably be more vulnerable than the front.

They turned the corner and took several steps—and a buzzer began to sound, loud and insistent. Stone halted and looked at them. "We tripped a wire somewhere. The fat's in the fire."

"Bloody hell," Loughlin said. "Let's get inside out of the cold."

Hog punched a hole in the glass of the nearest window, reached in, unlatched it and opened it. He cupped both hands over one knee and Loughlin placed his foot there and was hoisted up. He slid inside in a moment and grinned down at them. "It's a pantry. Anyone hungry?"

# Chapter Twelve

Stone went in next, then they pulled Hog up. It was a neatly organized pantry, as they could see in the dim light; there were two doors. One gave onto a narrow hall.

Buzzers were sounding all through the house and they could hear running footsteps and distant shouts. With every passing minute, their chances of getting out alive with Neff were getting slimmer. It was time to look to their own survival.

With Hog leading, they went down the hall and came to a T-shaped intersection. To the left was a closed, locked door that looked very solid. To the right was a smallish, well-furnished reading room; the walls were all bookcases, filled with books. The room was dark. They crossed it and opened another door cautiously; it gave onto a wide plant-and-flower-bedecked area that looked to be fifty yards long, roofed with glass.

Three men were gathered at the far end, one with a rifle. None of them looked like Neff.

Suddenly, the buzzers were turned off. The resulting stillness was somehow more ominous. The men separated and one came straight toward them, pushing a magazine clip into a pistol. He pulled the slide back and turned his head this way and that, as if expecting to find enemies in the plants.

Stone left the door ajar and the man opened it wide, extending his arm with the gun. Stone chopped his wrist and the pistol dropped. Hog backhanded the man and Loughlin caught him as he fell. But Hog had hit him too hard. He was dead before he reached the floor.

"Damn," Hog said. "Now he can't tell us nothing."

They laid the body in a corner behind an easy chair where it might not be noticed.

"Neff doesn't live on this floor," Stone said. "He must be upstairs."

Loughlin remarked, "If they find any of these bodies Hog is providing us with, they're going to send for reinforcements."

"That's right. But it'll take a bit of time. . . ."

"We passed some doors back there," Hog said. "Let's go open 'em. We might find some stairs."

"Good idea," Stone agreed.

There were stairs behind one of them, very narrow and dark. They also creaked and there was a landing where the steps made a sharp turn. A tiny round grimy-glassed window provided enough light to see by. At the top was a door that opened to their touch. They stepped into an unused bedchamber. It contained dusty furniture, chairs and end tables, but no bed. It had no bathroom attached. A house this size, Stone thought, must contain a dozen bedrooms . . . or more.

The house seemed silent. Stone opened the only other door and found it led into another bedchamber. This one held a made-up bed and looked recently used. There was an armoire with men's clothes in it. Another door opened onto a wide bare room devoid of furniture. It was nearly square and the windows had no curtains or draperies. There were wooden plaques on the walls with coats of arms.

They crossed the room and found a narrow hallway— and could hear voices. Men were arguing. Loughlin listened and reported they were discussing the alarm, some saying it was nothing, others that they must take every precaution.

Loughlin said, "They haven't found any bodies yet."

Stone asked, "Is one of them Neff?"

"I can't tell. They're not using names."

"Even if they do detect us, they probably won't look on

this floor for us. Let's search the rest of the rooms."

The men's voices faded.

To the right of the hall were rooms, seemingly built in no particular plan; all were empty. Some had furniture that was sheeted. It was an unused area of the big house.

In the middle of the house was a staircase leading down, and another leading up. Stone looked up into darkness, debating whether or not to go up—and suddenly shouts came from below them on the ground floor.

Loughlin took several steps down the stairs and looked around at them. "They've found the body in the room."

Stone said, "Now they'll search the house. Let's not make it easy for them." He moved toward the front. "We'll have to go out a window."

As they moved, men spilled up the stairs from below. Hog watched them from the shadows; they hurried to the back of the house, a half dozen, carrying pistols and rifles.

He said to Stone, "While they're snoopin' around the back, whyn't we go down them stairs?"

Stone grinned. "Yeah . . . why not?"

But halfway down, a bullet spanged against the banister. Loughlin fired back and they took the steps three at a time. Another shot, fired in haste, smashed a glass door behind them.

They were at the far end of the same glass-roofed arboretum they'd seen before. To the right was a huge room with chairs and couches and a massive fireplace at the far end. Stone jogged through it and paused at the door to a foyer.

There was a large circular room with doors opening off it, and the front door of the house. It had leaded glass decorations around it; there were plants in the round room and bright lights outside the door. They could hear a truck engine starting up. "We go out the front door," Stone said. "We shoot out the lights and move to the right. Okay?"

"Gotcha, neighbor." Hog nodded.

Stone waited till the truck rumbled away. Then he stepped up to the heavy door. Instantly several shots cracked and the glass in the door splintered. Stone sagged against the door for a moment. Loughlin jumped in front of him and fired a long burst from the Uzi as Hog grabbed Stone and hustled him through the door.

Outside, Hog shot out the nearest arc light. Loughlin shot out the others. Glass sprinkled the grass and it was suddenly dark. Stone grunted, "I'm all right . . ."

"Where you hit?"

"In the left arm."

Hog said, "Hell, you got another'n." He looked around the corner of the house, lifted the Uzi and shot out another light.

His burst brought several answering shots from the dark, quick blossoms of flame. Loughlin reloaded the Uzi and sprayed the spot. Someone fired from a window above them, five shots that came nowhere near.

Stone squeezed off three rounds from his Walther at the window. "Let's go."

They ran into the field, and in a few minutes, a truck halted and a searchlight clicked on and began to move across the weeds. Hog halted. "What you figger . . . a hunnerd yards?"

"About that," Loughlin said.

Hog aimed the Uzi and fired a burst. The light went out and someone yelled.

Hog chuckled. "About a hunnerd and ten."

No more lights came on. They moved in the direction they'd come from originally and Stone called for the chopper to meet them in the same spot it had dropped them.

They entered the woods, with one last look behind them. Lights were coming on again around the house, and they could see considerable bustle—but there was no pursuit. They paid no attention to the little green wires, went through the fence, and in a dozen minutes the chopper appeared.

Carol Jenner met them and Meydel in the brick-lined room. She had already been to the infirmary and watched the doctor fuss over Stone's wound.

Meydel mumbled appropriate words.

Stone grunted, "It was a bust for us. You can't win 'em all."

"Did you see Karl Neff at all?"

"No. Or the girl, Ullman, either." Stone sighed deeply. "But we alerted them that we know about Reinsburg."

Carol nodded. "We've got people watching it. If they move out we'll follow. Did anyone see any of you—could you tell?"

Loughlin shook his head. "I don't think anyone—"

"Two of them saw Hog," Stone interrupted. "But we're not sure they'll be able to talk about it for a while—or ever." He pantomimed knocking heads together. "Someone may have seen me at the door, but only from the back."

Meydel asked, "How many of them were there?"

Stone looked at the others. "Maybe ten?"

"Ten or twelve," Loughlin agreed.

"Minus one'r two," Hog said. "But they know it was us. They's no chance of convincin' them it was burglars."

Carol nodded sadly. "I suppose so."

Meydel remarked, "At least it's keeping them occupied. If they are making plans against the secretary, they'll have to take these three gentlemen into account."

"Thanks for the 'gentlemen.'" Hog smiled at the little man. "I ain't been called that in a long time."


Karl Neff was astonished and thoroughly frightened by the sudden attack on the house. A burst of fire had missed him by inches and he had pissed his pants while scrambling for safety.

For long minutes he had lain in a dark corner, smelling dust, his eyes tightly closed as if it would make him invisible.

Then the attackers were gone, as suddenly as they had come, and he got to his feet shakily. He had never before been so close to death. While the others were tending to security, he made his way to his apartment and changed clothes. Then, after a hearty drink, he went downstairs to shout at Johann Dicot.

"How were they able to get into this house?"

"They broke a window and—"

"I mean, how were they able to get close to it?" Neff pounded on a chair arm. "Have we no security?"

"If we put out the necessary security there will be talk in the village. We cannot hide the dogs and—"

"Electronics!" shouted Neff. "There must be a way!"

"We have an electronic beam close to the house. It is what alerted us." The stocky Dicot faced the other, hands on hips. His dark face was screwed into a scowl. "We have done everything we were allowed."

Neff took a long breath, sighing, a hand over his eyes. "Very well, Johann. A thing like this is . . . very upsetting. See that the damage is repaired."

"Will you stay here after this?"

Neff did not answer for a moment. Then he nodded. "Yes, I think so. For the moment, anyway. I must make a report. We will see what comes of that."

Dicot nodded and went out to give his orders.

Neff closed his eyes. So Carlo Vanner had not been able to contain the three Americans. . . . He almost smiled. Von Schiller could make mistakes just as anyone could. In his private opinion, Vanner was overrated by von Schiller.

He went to his desk and began to write his report. He would make it as bland as possible, but he knew von Schiller's response would be to vacate the estate. He was sure of that. The Frankfurt police would become very interested in the place. And von Schiller would say it had outlived its usefulness.

Well, so be it. He rather hated to leave; the big house was comfortable.

He finished the report to von Schiller and sealed it in an envelope. Then he made several telephone calls and had the little dumpy man, Danzig, brought to him.

Danzig wore a wrinkled and stained suit with burn holes in the sleeves. He looked like a bum. Neff stared sternly at the man. "Have you done as I asked?"

Danzig nodded quickly. "I have a full report on her, Herr Neff. I know all about her."

"And have you fixed a time and date?"

"I only await your command, sir."

Neff nodded. The little man was efficient, despite his looks. He had done well in the matter of Gerd Helbing. "Then you can carry out your orders at any time?"

*"Jawohl,* Herr Neff."

"Then do it at once—at the earliest opportunity."

Danzig smiled.

Neff fixed his eyes on the man. "Do not fail."

"I will not fail, Herr Neff." The little man erased the smile. "By this time tomorrow she will be dead."

# Chapter Thirteen

Frieda Jung was stationed in Frankfurt as a deputy assistant to the West German president, in charge of various matters, protocol among them. It was her job to arrange all the thousands of details concerning foreign visitors—security, housing, entertainment, as well as interpreters, other communications and transportation. At such times she was vastly overworked because she had difficulty delegating authority, insisted on overseeing everything her aides did, and carried much of the detail in her head.

She was thus a liability—and indispensable.

Her loss would upset the government considerably, as was reported to Karl Neff. It might shake them up almost as much as the death of Gerd Helbing had done. Those ramifications were still being felt.

The report about Frieda Jung indicated that it would probably take half a dozen to replace her and that the job they did would be less efficient.

Danzig had managed the surveillance on her, received the various reports and checked them, exactly as he had done with the Helbing case, before sending them on. He knew her associates and her habits, and in a sense it had been easier than with Helbing.

Frieda was a woman who stayed within schedules whenever possible despite the heavy demands of her work. And when she had no VIPs to care for, her work schedule was exact; she seldom varied from a routine. These habits made it easy for Danzig to pick his spot and the day.

For the actual elimination, Danzig had decided upon a young man named Thomas Emden. Emden was twenty-five, had spent several years in prison and had no apparent morals or nerves. He was a mild-looking individual who dressed carelessly and was unshaven much of the time. He looked like an out-of-work idler—which he was.

But he had much experience with weapons and, in prison, had learned about electronics. He was good with his hands. Danzig had sent out word to his underworld contacts and several had suggested Emden for dangerous work.

Emden had called him "sir" when they met. They sat in an alehouse and Danzig smoked two packs of cigarettes while they talked. He thought Emden would do.

He told Emden of the route Frieda Jung always took from her office in the Ministry building to the parking lot, where she had a space with her name on it. Her car was a light blue American Chevrolet.

It was a large parking lot, serving three or four public buildings. Walking through it later Emden asked, "Is she always alone?"

"Almost always. If she is not, we will postpone until the next day."

Emden wanted to see the route she would walk, and went over it several times. He looked at the surrounding buildings and asked about times.

"She comes out of that door," Danzig indicated, "at five-thirty, as regular as clockwork. It will not yet be dark."

He also supplied Emden with half a dozen photos of Jung. She was a distinctive-looking woman, slim and angular. She always wore tailored suits, sometimes a topcoat, and always carried an attaché case.

Danzig drove Emden to look at Frieda Jung's apartment house. They followed her home and watched her put the Chevrolet into a small garage and go into the building.

Then Emden asked, "Do you have a preference in the way it is to be done, sir?"

Danzig shook his head. "You are the expert. I leave it to you. We only want the obituary notice."

"Very well."

The next morning it rained, but the afternoon was clear and slightly chilly with a cold, steady wind.

Danzig picked up Emden at his run-down hotel. They drove to the lot late in the afternoon. Emden was dressed as a worker, with a shapeless cap and overalls. He walked into the lot with a small toolbox and smoked several cigarettes, moving about aimlessly, making sure the lot was vacant of prying eyes.

Then he stopped at the blue Chevrolet and spent twenty minutes with his wiring and the sticks of explosive.

Danzig, smoking furiously, was parked outside the lot and slightly above it on a city street. With his binoculars he watched the Ministry door and Emden at the automobile. A few people went in and out of the building but none went near the car.

Emden returned to Danzig's car and they sat patiently, with Danzig lighting one cigarette from the butt of the last, till the street was sprinkled with little white butts.

And as always, on the dot, Frieda Jung came from the door and strode across the lot to her car. Danzig watched, fascinated, as Emden opened the lid of a small black metal box on his lap. Jung unlocked the car and slid under the wheel, slamming the door.

Emden closed a switch.

Instantly the distant car went up in a huge orange explosion. The sound reached them in another second; the concussion rocked the car. Danzig hunched his shoulders at the sheer force of it. Black smoke curled upward and bits and pieces of the car rained down, cluttering the yard.

Staring at the blackened space through his binocs, Danzig swore softly in German. Then he nodded, hearing distant sirens. "Very good, Thomas." He started the engine. "Very good." He turned on the car lights and they drove away slowly.

He took Emden several miles away to his slum section

of town. He would leave Frankfurt the next morning, he told Danzig. He would go to Spain and spend some of the money he had just earned.

"A splendid idea," Danzig said. "I would go there myself if I could get away."

Danzig parked the car around the corner from Emden's cheap hotel and cut the lights. "Give me an address where you can be reached. I may have another job for you."

Emden patted his overall pockets. "I have nothing to write with."

"There's paper and pencil in the glove compartment."

As Emden opened it, Danzig pushed an automatic pistol into his side and fired four quick shots. Then he took back the money he had given Emden, opened the car door and pushed the body out.

News of the assassination of Frieda Jung was on the radio minutes after the event. It was not known for a time whether or not anyone had been in the car; the explosion had been devastating. Nothing was left of the Chevrolet, and seven other automobiles were also destroyed.

But Frieda Jung's habits were well known and she had been seen leaving her office—it had to be assumed she had been killed in the blast.

The media speculated on why she had been killed, and no one had an answer. No one telephoned the police to claim responsibility.

Danzig listened to the radio as he drove back across town. It had all gone very smoothly. As he had promised Karl, he had not failed.

There was nothing to connect this latest atrocity to Karl Neff but, as Carol Jenner said, it had his stamp. A hard blow had been struck, unexpectedly, and no clues had been left behind. In fact there was nothing at all but the huge blackened area the television stations were showing.

Later, the news reported that a body with four bullets fired at close range had been found, but no connection was made by the police between that occurrence and the explosion that had killed the woman, Jung.

"But it does resemble the shooting of Webster Rankin," Stone said. "The executioner is executed. How many times was Rankin shot?"

"Four times," Carol replied. "That *is* a coincidence, isn't it? . . . I wonder if the police noticed it."

"Ask them for a rundown on the man who was shot," Stone suggested.

"I will."

Carol was able to get that information over the telephone. The dead man's name had been Thomas Emden; born in Berlin of German mother and Belgian father. He had served two prison terms, both for armed robbery, and had been suspected of half a dozen crimes the police could not prove.

He was unmarried, and lived in a sleazy hotel only a few steps from where he'd been murdered. The police theorized that the murderer had driven him home and shot him. His body had been found in the gutter; the police theory was that it had been pushed from a car.

The police were investigating, attempting to question Emden's friends—if he'd had any.

"He sounds like exactly the right man to blow up Frieda Jung," Loughlin said.

"And get shot for his trouble," Carol agreed.

"So it's the chain-smoker again—maybe," Stone said, scratching his jaw. "Why did he hire someone to blow up the girl—because he didn't know how to do it?"

"Possible." Loughlin nodded. "Of course, he could have shot the girl."

"Maybe no nerve," Hog said.

"But he shot the man who shot Helbing."

"At touch range," Loughlin remarked. "He couldn't miss. He couldn't miss in the car either. He doesn't trust himself at a distance."

"Well," Carol said, "he's got the money to hire people. At least, he has to show it to them. So far he hasn't paid any of it out . . . that we know. We've had no luck finding out who's behind Neff. He's still at Reinsburg, by the way."

"How long had Emden lived here in Frankfurt?" Stone asked.

Carol shook her head. "They promised me more info tomorrow."

But when tomorrow came they had very little more information for her. Evidently Emden had been a solitary man. No one in the hotel knew him except by sight. His records said he'd come to Frankfurt from Berlin, but the address the Berlin police had for him was also kaput. A new building stood on the spot. His parents could not be found. It was as if he had never existed.

"Perfect for the job," Stone remarked.

"But the police did tell me one thing more," Carol said.

"What?"

"They think they know the name of the man who chainsmoked and who killed Webster Rankin . . . and possibly this one, Emden."

"Oh? What is it?"

"Danzig."

"Danzig? That's the name of a city."

She said, "Danzig was living with a woman who began to be suspicious of him and went to discuss it with her brother, a policeman. The brother went to his captain with the story and Danzig proved to have a record. They're looking for him."

"That's the whole name—Danzig?"

"It's all they would tell me. They were reluctant to give me that much. You know how cops are."

"Did the woman he lived with happen to have a photo of Danzig?"

"No, but I have a description. He's a dumpy little man, not much to look at. Big nose, pig eyes . . . and he chainsmokes, which you already know. He is a German but he speaks English very well."

Loughlin said, "That description might fit about ten thousand men in this city. What does he do for a living?"

Carol said, "They didn't tell me."

Meydel said, "It is probably not his real name. He must have underworld connections to be able to hire these men

—at least to hire Emden." He looked at Carol. "Let us put out feelers in that direction."

"Yes. If he goes by that name, it is unusual enough. . . ."

# Chapter Fourteen

Odile Buchon had been brought up in Alsace and spoke German as well as French. The French police had been watching her closely, but not closely enough, and she had fled to Frankfurt, where she had once lived, to pick up the pieces again.

But trouble and Odile were sisters. She was drunk and disorderly when the police collected her, along with several others, and shoved them all into a smelly tank with no consideration for gender.

And in the tank Odile got herself into a biting, scratching fight with another woman and had much of her shirtwaist torn to shreds, allowing twin assets to show. These were noted at once by several males not as drunk as others, and Odile was fair game during the night, raped continually, her protests stifled.

In the morning the inmates of the tank were brought out one by one, their names and addresses written down, and most were sent on their way.

But when Odile gave her name she was taken at once to a separate room and allowed to clean herself up and handed a blouse. A quiet, understanding policeman listened to her protests and she was questioned again about the Gerd Helbing affair. By this time she was feeling very sorry for herself and at last confided to a sympathetic ear that she had not yet been paid for her part in that incident.

Perhaps if she had been herself and not still woozy from

the effects of drink, and the degradation of the rapes, she would not have uttered the fateful words.

They caused a mild sensation among the detectives of the force. Who owed her money? Was it Karl Neff?

Odile held out against them for an hour or more, till they wore her down. Yes, it was Karl Neff. Yes, she had been his lover for a time. No, she did not see him anymore. Her calls to him went unanswered. No, she had not known that Helbing was to be killed that day. Neff had told her nothing.

Did she know a man called Danzig?

No, she did not.

Her story leaked out to the press and the entire murder of Gerd Helbing was gone over again with headlines and lurid drawings and Odile Buchon's statement that she had not been paid for her part in it.

The newspapers dug up photographs of a half-naked Odile and printed them happily with many speculations.

Hog examined the papers with interest. "I told you she had great tits."

"Well, Karl Neff is going to beat on them with a stick. Her mouth is too big," Loughlin said.

But Stone doubted she had done Neff much harm. "With her background any lawyer could tear her statement to shreds. There's no proof of anything. It's her word against his."

"The tits oughta count for somethin'," Hog protested. "If *I* was the judge . . ." He shrugged.

"Yes, you'd make a wonderful judge," Loughlin commented. "I read somewhere that Anne Boleyn had six tits. Did you know that?"

"Hell," Hog said, "I woulda never let them chop her head off."

Neff read the papers and watched the newscasters on television and was furious about the Odile Buchon "exposé." She had brought his name into the affair. He knew how that would set with von Schiller.

And he was right. Von Schiller's call was icy and sarcastic. He said his few, steely words and hung up without allowing Neff to reply.

Neff then made the decision he had been putting off. He would move from Reinsburg. He sent men out. "Find us another place." He did not ask von Schiller; he did not want to talk to von Schiller for a while.

As far as Odile was concerned, what did she know? She had known that Helbing was to be at her apartment at a particular time, but she did not know that Danzig and a sniper were in the building across the street. She had told the police that she had given that information to Karl Neff ... but he could say she had not, that she was only trying to get publicity for herself. And the way the newspapers and magazines were using her undressed pictures, it bolstered his story.

No, he had nothing to fear from her. Perhaps it would have been simpler in the long run to have sent her the few francs he had promised. . . .

The police had come to Reinsburg at once, after the three Americans had raided, but they had not found him or anything of an accusing nature. Reinsburg was very old and had several secret rooms. But it was annoying to have the police suddenly appear with their warrants. He would have to get out.

His men found another, smaller estate. It was on a stream with wide fields, a mile distant from the nearest neighbor, with a village five miles farther on. It was called Osten, after its builder. When he saw it, Neff leased it at once, under an assumed name.

Johann Dicot hired three moving vans to cart their belongings to the new place. One of the vans was owned by Ignaz Meyer, a short, muscular Bavarian who was in the pay of Carol Jenner's section.

Carol knew of the move as soon as it began.


The matter of Eva Ullman had been passed over by Karl Neff; he had other things on his mind. She had been locked in a room and forgotten. When he had time he would attend to her. He had not yet made up his mind what to do with her.

For her part, she thought of nothing but how to get away from him. When she heard about the move she was delighted. Maybe her chance would come.

But it did not. She was taken out of the room and put into a car and driven to Osten with hardly a word being said. She had a good look at the estate as they arrived, and from the windows of her second-story room she could see a good deal more, including the tops of distant houses—which she figured must be in the village.

There would be a telephone in the village.

Her windows were not barred. They were the kind that opened by means of a handle that one turned. When she tried it, she found that the rust had settled in and it was only with difficulty that she was able to open one halfway. But it was enough; she could squeeze out when the time came.

How would she get down to the grass below? It was too far to jump with safety. If she turned her ankle or broke a leg . . .

She thought of bed sheets tied together—she had seen that trick in the movies, but real life was another matter. Would the knots be secure enough? There was ivy on the outside wall but it did not look strong enough to hold a person; perhaps Robin Hood might be able to climb it—in the movies.

She examined the door. Someone had put on a lock, a round yellow brass affair that looked efficient. It would not give to a hairpin. However they did *that!*

So it had to be the window.

There were guards outside the house; she could see them patrolling at night, strolling in twos, smoking and talking. She timed them with her wristwatch. They came around the house about once an hour, sometimes a little longer. Once in a while, late at night, they came only once every two hours.

But she didn't need two hours. She could be in the village in an hour easily. But that late at night, would there be anyone up? She might have to hide herself till morning.

Could she steal a car and drive into Frankfurt?

First things first. She had to get out of the house. She

had some money in her purse, they had not taken it away from her. She might be able to hire a taxi. . . .

The day she decided to make the attempt was the longest of the year. The hours crept by with agonizing slowness. After they brought her the evening meal she lay on the bed, but it was impossible to sleep. She looked at the clock a thousand times.

But midnight finally came.

She had stood at the window for hours. The guards had strolled by, perhaps a hundred yards from the house, near eleven o'clock. At twelve-thirty they strolled by again.

As soon as they were out of sight, Eva pulled the sheets from the bed. She rolled them diagonally for length, tied them end to end, then tied one end around the metal windowframe, testing by pulling as hard as she could. Then she eased the sheets out the window and crawled out immediately without allowing herself to think about it.

It proved to be easier than she'd feared.

She let herself down as far as the sheets allowed, then dropped to the grass, only a few feet.

But when she looked up, the sheets hung there, a white slash against the dark building. She swore and ran lightly across the grass. There was nothing she could do about the sheets now.

She headed for the road, hurrying across the nearest field. It was very quiet; could they hear her panting? She was wearing low-heeled shoes and dark clothes. She was probably not easy to spot. She glanced back at the house. There were a few lights burning but it looked serene in the night.

So far there was no alarm.

She gained the road. It was unpaved and gravelly. She began to lope toward the village. The chances were that when they discovered she was missing they would not sound an alarm—it would alert her. They would probably fan out in all directions silently. And the first place they would look would be the village. The thought gave her a twinge.

But it was the place she had to go. She recalled it from the quick look she'd had in the car when they brought her there. It was small, a quaint-looking little place, almost medieval, probably a tourist attraction.

It took less than an hour to run the five miles to the village, and when she approached, she forced herself to walk slowly, regaining her breath. There was no one on the road behind her.

There was no one on the main street, but in the center of the town was a public telephone. She laid out all her coins and called the operator, asking for the Frankfurt police. When a man's voice replied she told him her name and where she was and said she was in great danger.

The voice conferred with someone else for a moment, then came back on the line. "Miss Ullman—there is a policeman in that town. Find him and stay with him and we will send someone for you at once."

She thanked him and hung up. Where would she find a policeman? There should be a station, shouldn't there? She jogged along the street looking for it.

She heard the motorcycle long before she saw it. It was approaching from the direction of Osten. Eva jumped into a deep doorway and pressed herself against one wall. The cycle went past slowly, and as he passed her she could see his head turning this way and that.

They had discovered her escape.

# Chapter Fifteen

Carol Jenner's superiors had arranged a communications channel between Operations and the police, so that when the police received the message from Eva Ullman, Operations was duly informed.

Stone, Loughlin and Wiley were routed out after midnight and told that Eva had contacted the police, and where she could be found. The village was called Kelber. They got a car from Jerry Conte in the motor pool and raced for it. With any luck they would reach the village before Karl Neff was submachine-gunning her on the main street.

"I told you she wasn't one of the gang," Loughlin said with satisfaction. "I don't believe she ever made that call to us."

Hog grinned. "You still hot for her after all these years?"

"Gentlemen don't talk about such things."

*"Men* do," Hog said. "What's with the 'gentlemen' stuff? Does that mean ya can't get it up?"

Loughlin sighed. "My mother would never approve of you."

Hog laughed.

Stone said, "Shut up, you two. Who's got the map?"

"Me," Hog said. He unfolded it. "The town's only got a couple streets. The main one and two cross streets. The population is about four thousand."

"There must be more than two cross streets."

"Well, there's some alleys and paths but they's no way to know how big they is. I mean, if we could get a car in."

Loughlin said, "Why don't we leave the car at the edge of town and slip in nice and quiet?"

"I vote the same way," Hog said, folding up the map. "The cop house is on the first cross street. Maybe she's there."

"If she isn't, she may be in deep shit."


Eva slipped out of the doorway when the motorcyclist had passed. She could tell by the motor when he turned and started back. She ducked into another doorway and stumbled on some dark steps. They led to the second floor and she went up quickly, trying to be silent. She came out on a walkway where there were several closed doors and a painted number on each.

At the end of the walk there were more stairs, leading down into a yard where several cars were parked. It was very dark and she had to feel her way down the steps. At the bottom she could see an alleyway that dived between two houses, the only way out for the cars. She went to it and found a slope down, treacherous in the gloom. When she reached the bottom she could hear the motorcycle again, and several automobiles.

But they were a block away. She was on a dirt road that seemed to circle the town. She passed occasional houses, none with lights, and when she heard the motorcycle noises grow louder, she ran into the field on her left and flopped full length on the ground.

The cyclist passed on the road and disappeared into the dark. Eva rose cautiously. Would she ever find the police?

She came to a cross street and halted. The street petered out into the fields. Toward the center of town were signs, all dark except one: POLIZEI. It was in blue neon and looked to be half a mile away. Could she reach it before they grabbed her?

As she watched, a car went by on the main street, moving slowly. She could almost feel the eyes searching, peering. . . .

Would they shoot her down when they found her?

She started along the street, moving very slowly, from one doorway to the next . . . and a car came up behind her. She slid behind a pillar, sure they had seen her, but the car went on by. Eva almost collapsed in a heap, her heart beating wildly.

She was in a dark and wide doorway; there were two doors and the pillar between them. She leaned against its cold surface, afraid to move. She was trembling all over.

As they approached the village of Kelber, Stone slowed the car. He pulled it into the deep shadow of a row of trees and stopped. "End of the line."

They slid out, closing the car doors silently. "She was told to go to the police station and stay there," Stone said, "so we can look there first, right?"

"Righto. Very logical."

Hog asked, "How many cops in this burg?"

"One, I think," Stone said. He led at a fast walk to the nearest building. The town ended abruptly at a stone bridge.

Hog said, "Now where the hell is that girl?"

"She phoned from here," Stone said. "She's probably holed up somewhere."

"Hope she's protectin' them tits. Be a shame to—"

"Jesus!" Loughlin shook his head. "There's more to life than tits."

"There is?" Hog looked surprised.

"Will you two shut up," Stone growled. "How'll we find the girl?"

"Start yelling?" Hog asked. "Hey, Eva, where the hell are you?"

Loughlin chuckled. "Maybe that's as good a way as any."

"All right." Stone pointed at the center of the road. "You tell your name and see if she hears."

Loughlin walked to the middle of the street. He shouted: "Eva—it's Terry. Where are you?"

He shouted half a dozen times. Several people opened windows to look, and lights went on. A middle-aged man came out of the police station carrying a shotgun.

In the midst of the turmoil Hog noticed the girl who came from the darkness of the side street. He pointed her out to Stone and Loughlin. The Brit exclaimed, "That's Eva!" He ran to her.

She almost collapsed into his arms. She was white and trembling and clung to him like a drowning person. Loughlin picked her up and carried her away from the noise and confusion.

Hog brought the car and they put her into it. She was cold, and Loughlin wrapped her in his coat as Stone wheeled the car around the town on the dirt road, then crossed the bridge and headed for Frankfurt.

# Chapter Sixteen

Danzig had moved to Osten along with the others, and was given a small room on the second floor. He had been given a bonus by Neff after the Frieda Jung operation and he was eager to spend it in Berlin.

He was making plans to go there when he received the phone call. A strange voice said to him: "You are to come to the Club Heppe at midnight tonight. Be outside the door at precisely twelve."

"Who is this?"

"I am Carlo Vanner."

Danzig recognized the name. Vanner was an aide to von Schiller! He said, "I will be there."

Vanner hung up.

Danzig lit a cigarette and considered. Certainly Vanner did not want to see him. It must be von Schiller! Perhaps another job to do. Why else would von Schiller send for him? Danzig smiled. Perhaps he was moving up in the organization. His talents were being recognized at last.

He slept several hours during the day and that night he asked to borrow a car to drive into Frankfurt.

Johann asked him, "What for?"

Vanner had not told him to say nothing, but Danzig's native caution did. "I've got money to spend."

"Are you a drinking man?"

"No. Why?"

"We don't want a bigmouth in any beer hall. . . . Do you know a girl there in town?"

Danzig hesitated, then he nodded.

Johann stared at him for a moment, then arranged for a car to be brought. When Danzig had left, Johann went to see Neff.

"How far do we trust the potato face?"

"Danzig? What is it?"

"He's just now gone into the city. He says he wants to spend some of his money." Johann frowned. "I don't know why, but I don't believe him."

"What do you think?"

"I think he's gone to see someone. He got a telephone call from the city earlier."

"A girl?"

Johann shook his head. "Girls don't flock to the potato face. He has to buy them. I think it's something else."

"Go on."

"What does Danzig do for a living? He manages killings." Johann frowned and hunched his shoulders. "Someone wants to hire him. Who, do you suppose?"

Neff studied the other. "Only a few of us know what Danzig does. One of them is von Schiller. Is it possible the call was from him?"

"It is very possible."

"I suppose we'll hear about it sooner or later. . . ."

After Johann had left, Neff thought about it. A curious occurrence. Johann was right, girls never called Danzig . . . never wanted him around, unless he paid them for their favors.

Did von Schiller want someone dead?

Neff had received the impression that von Schiller was very unhappy with him. Could it be himself that von Schiller was interested in erasing? The general was fully capable of snuffing out an unwanted life in a second, without a moment's consideration. He was utterly ruthless . . . which was how he'd gotten where he was.

Was there anyone who could easily take his place here at Osten?

That thought made him very uneasy. Yes, there were

several. Johann Dicot, for one. And doubtless von Schiller could name half a dozen.

What could he do about it? For one thing he could grill Danzig when he returned. There were ways to make the potato face talk.

Danzig was met promptly at midnight in front of the Club Heppe. He did not enter the club but was put into a long black car and driven away. The man on the seat beside him was Carlo Vanner.

In reply to Danzig's question, Vanner said, "Von Schiller will tell you himself what he wants. I am merely delivering you."

Danzig smoked three cigarettes before the car turned into a long, dark drive and halted at a side door. He got out with Vanner and looked at a huge stone house surrounded by ghostly trees, with only a few glimmering lights showing. Vanner led him up a flight of stairs and unlocked a door.

He pointed to a bowl. "Put out your cigarette and don't light any in von Schiller's presence. He can't stand them."

Sighing, Danzig did as he was told. He followed Vanner through several rooms to a large sitting room with an immense fieldstone fireplace that was blazing merrily. Von Schiller, tall and gray, stood before it, warming his backside. He stared at Danzig as Vanner announced him, then nodded and pointed to a chair.

Vanner left the room and Danzig sat, reaching for a cigarette, then remembering. He twiddled his fingers. Von Schiller still stared at him as if he were something from outer space.

Then von Schiller said, "You come well recommended."

"Thank you, sir."

"I am told you do not actually pull the trigger yourself."

Danzig shrugged. "That depends, sir."

"I mean of course concerning the main victim. Helbing, for instance."

"Yes, that is so, sir. Of course, there was another circumstance regarding Herr Helbing."

Von Schiller nodded. "We wished to throw suspicion on the Americans. You could have disposed of Frieda Jung yourself."

"I am not an expert with guns or explosives, sir. When I am given the order I see that it is carried out exactly. The persons who do this work are often under some influence, drugs or alcohol, and can be led to talk about it later. I make certain this is not the case."

"You are an interesting specimen, Danzig. I have never known another murder broker."

Danzig shifted uncomfortably.

"Well," von Schiller said, "to business. I have a case for you. A person must be removed from office, as it were." He made a peculiar sound in his throat and Danzig realized the man was chuckling.

"Yes, sir?"

"I will not tell you how I wish this to be done. That is your province . . . but I would rather it not be as spectacular as the death of Fraülein Jung. The media make too much of it. It puts pressure on the police to perform . . . you understand."

"Yes, sir."

"I wish this job to be done soon and you are to speak of it with no one. No one at all." Von Schiller fixed him with a steely gaze and Danzig gritted his teeth. Jesus! He wanted a cigarette!

"I understand, sir."

"Very well."

"Who is the man, sir?"

"Karl Neff."

Danzig left the room vastly surprised. He had never considered Karl as a possibility and in truth was a bit shocked at the idea. But of course that had nothing to do with his professional ethics. The job as contracted for would be carried out.

Carlo Vanner had other surprises for him. "You will not be going back to Osten."

"Why not?"

"It is not your decision," Vanner said coldly. "You are

under orders. You will be going to Berlin very soon. In the meantime you will remain here. The car will be returned."

"But why will I go to Berlin? Do you know what I am to do?"

"Of course I know. Come along. I will show you to your quarters." On the way up the stairs, Vanner said, "I would do the job myself, but von Schiller has set me another task."

"But . . . Berlin!"

Vanner stopped at a door. "This is your room." He turned the knob and they went in to a very pleasant large room with a bathroom attached. He said, "Neff will be sent to Berlin in the next several days."

"Ah, I see."

Eva Ullman had not been harmed; she had been frightened to death, but a good night's sleep and the feeling of safety were all she needed. Karl Neff, she told them, was a cold-blooded killer, and so were his men. Men like Danzig, for instance.

"Tell us about Danzig," Stone asked.

"Killing is his job," Eva replied. "I am positive he managed the Helbing affair and killed Webster Rankin. And I think he also had Frieda Jung killed. He is a dumpy little man; anyone would think him to be a shabby little book-keeper to look at him. I don't know how many he killed before Helbing."

She drew them a plan of Osten and answered questions about the estate. She could tell them nothing about Neff's plans for the future. In fact, she seldom saw him since Britt Gericke had taken her place in his affections. She had been a virtual prisoner in the house ever since she had seen Terry Loughlin in the warehouse and had uttered his name.

She had never been able to explain that to Neff's satisfaction.

She was positive he thought her a government agent.

She also knew there was someone who was superior to Neff, but she had no idea who it was. "They sometimes spoke of him as 'the general,'" she said. "I got the impression he supplied them with money."

"Does their organization have a name?" Stone asked.

"I don't know." She shook her head, thinking about it. "If it does, I never heard it. What are you going to do with me?"

"We want you to stay here for the time being. It depends on what happens to Karl Neff—I mean, whether or not you testify in his case."

"What happens to him?"

Stone said, "We're trying to bring him in."

"Yes, I heard the shooting when you got into Reinsburg. I was locked in a room on the third floor." She smiled. "Afterward they were furious."

"We kicked their butts," Hog said.

Carol asked, "Did you call Terry Loughlin on the telephone and make an appointment with him?"

Loughlin added, "Soon after I saw you at the warehouse with Neff."

Eva shook her head again. "No. I was never allowed near a telephone. It might have been Britt."

"It was definitely not you?"

"Absolutely not."

Stone had an aide take Eva to her quarters; she needed rest and sleep still; her nerves were still taut. This would be her last job in the field, she told them. Now she was ready for a desk in a quiet office.

Carol left them alone, to study the plans of Osten Eva had drawn for them. It was a much smaller estate than Reinsburg. There were four roads leading to the house; two went through the fields. There was a detached garage, a barnlike structure that Eva had not been in, and a number of sheds and minor buildings.

Still, it was not a small house. Eva had not been in all the rooms and could only guess at most. She had been held on the second floor and had escaped through the window.

Stone said, "By now they know Eva got away, of course. If the police do not show up at Osten and search, will Neff and his men figure we grabbed her?"

"Probably," Loughlin agreed.

"So they'll be looking for us to show up at Osten?"

"I think so." Loughlin smiled. "We are, aren't we?"

Stone nodded. "I wish there were some way we could be certain Neff will be there."

"Not bloody likely."

"What about the informer Carol said she has inside the organization?"

"Good show! Let's go ask her."

But the informer had not been heard from for a week or more, Carol told them. "He may not be able to get a message out. It can't be easy with everyone looking at everyone else. We can only wait and hope he's not been discovered."

"Maybe Hog shot him," Loughlin suggested.

"I'm gonna hold back yore grits," Hog growled.

Later that day, a pilot flew over the Osten estate in his chopper and a photographer took pictures that Stone and his men studied in the brick-lined room. They learned very little more than what Eva Ullman had told them.

The main house was definitely smaller than Reinsburg and would probably be easier to approach. But they could depend on the fact that the occupants had beefed up security. After they reached the house they might find it impossible to enter without alerting everyone for a mile around.

Bringing in Karl Neff was not going to be easy.

# Chapter Seventeen

The American secretary of state, Mr. Charles Ruston, was away from his office with a slight illness, according to the press secretary. However, at the end of a week the secretary was in the hospital and his condition was announced as more serious.

The press, sensing a big story, wormed its way in and came out with the news that Secretary Ruston had an inoperable form of cancer and probably would not leave the hospital.

When this news was circulated the White House was forced to admit it. All travel plans then became a thing of the past.

And all the elaborate plans von Schiller had made were also abandoned.

Karl Neff had been ordered to Berlin ostensibly to discuss the taking of the American official. He was housed on Bodmer Strasse in the home of one of von Schiller's aides —who was not privy to his superior's decision about Neff.

When Ruston's condition was made known, Neff requested permission to return to Osten but was told to remain for discussions concerning another American official. There were several American ambassadors in Europe, any one of whom might be targeted.

Neff made himself comfortable and waited. But the call did not come. When he telephoned von Schiller he was told that the general was deep in another matter and would see him as soon as it became possible.

Danzig was given the address on Bodmer Strasse, as well as the plan of the house, which was an apartment above a bakery. The aide whose house it was had been detached for an assignment in Belgium. The job would keep him there until Danzig had finished.

Danzig's first thought was to go to the house alone, knock on the door and, when Neff opened it, to shoot him in the head. The doorway of the house was recessed, at the top of a flight of stairs that was open to the air. He could have the pistol in his hand as he rapped on the door; no one would be able to see it from below.

But that method was not foolproof. Who was in the house with Neff? Johann Dicot, for instance, might come to the door.

He found a spot where he could sit in the car and see the door Neff would have to come through.

Carol heard from the informer inside Karl Neff's organization. He had only a moment to telephone her, he said. Neff was in Berlin, probably to see the general. There were three possible addresses: one address was on Leitschuk Strasse, another on Norte Strasse, the third on Bodmer Strasse.

"It's the best we can do," Carol told Stone and his men. "Neff may not be at any of them, but they're the only leads we've got."

"And that makes them worth checking out," Stone grunted. "Next stop: Berlin."

Danzig was rewarded by the sight of Karl Neff coming down the wooden steps to the street. He opened a garage door and backed out a small Japanese car and drove away. Danzig followed, puffing furiously.

Neff drove several miles to a large restaurant, where he met a man in a checked jacket and the two had dinner together as Danzig ate boiled eggs and drank beer across the room.

The two men had heads together for an hour or more and covered scraps of paper with writing; it was impossible to tell what they were discussing. Danzig had never seen the guy in the checked jacket before. He remained in the restaurant when Neff said goodbye and went out to the small car.

Danzig scrambled after him, but had no chance of a shot on the busy street. He would have to get up close to Neff to make sure. Danzig's hand shook too much to try a long shot of even twenty feet.

Neff drove at once to another part of town, parked the car on a street bright with neon and went into what looked to be a saloon. Danzig remained in his car, puffing on a cigarette. He had almost decided to follow Neff inside, when the other came out with a girl on his arm. Neff escorted her to the car; they both got in and Neff drove back to the apartment on Bodmer Strasse.

Neff had hired himself a hooker.

This would be an excellent time to sneak into the apartment—while Neff was occupied. But Danzig shook his head. He was no burglar. He didn't know how to break in silently. Finally, he gave up the idea.

Later in the afternoon Danzig followed Neff to another house and waited. When Neff came out he drove to a second house, where he picked up a short, slim man and went with him to a shopping center. The slim man went into one of the markets and came out with groceries, which he put into the little Japanese car. Then he and Neff drove back to Bodmer Strasse.

Neff had hired a cook.

Did that mean he was staying in the city for a time?

Danzig thought very seriously about whether this was the time. He had no silencer with him. It was that fact that finally decided him not to try.

In the morning Neff went out again in the small Japanese car. This time he drove to the airport and met a man who was getting ready to board a plane. Danzig stood just outside the large waiting room and smoked as he watched them talk.

As the passengers began boarding the plane, the two men stopped talking and Neff came out of the room, walking rapidly. Danzig had to turn his back and pretend interest in a window as Neff passed him. That had been too close for comfort since Neff was bound to recognize him.

But apparently he had not. He walked out to his car and drove away. Danzig followed at a distance.

That night Danzig watched the lights of the house go out one by one, except one. It was a warm spring night and he had the car window down.

Karl Neff came out of the house by the front door and walked around the row into the mews. He was wearing soft-soled shoes and dark clothes. He came up behind Danzig's car without a sound. Danzig was slumped, a burning cigarette in his fingers.

Neff extended his arm and, with the silenced pistol he had purchased that day, fired four shots into the dumpy little man.

He wiped the gun off and left it on the seat and went back into the house carrying Danzig's pistol.

With Stone driving, the three reached the Bodmer address and parked the car as Karl Neff came out of the house. It was late and man looked furtive. He walked quickly to the end of the row of buildings and disappeared. Hog jumped out and followed.

When he reached the mews, Hog saw Neff climb the back steps to the house and let himself in.

When the door closed, Hog went back to the car. "He just went around and up the steps into the goddamn house again."

"A constitutional?" Loughlin said.

"Not much of a walk." Stone shook his head. "Why would he do a thing like that? Did he meet anyone in the back?"

"Nobody. Maybe he left a message for somebody, though."

"If he did," Stone said gloomily, "we'd never find it in the dark."

"We know he's in the house," Loughlin said. "Let's go get him."

"Right," Stone agreed. "Hog stays in front; we go in the back." He grabbed Hog's arm. "We want him alive."

Hog grunted. "Did you tell him that?"

"I'll tell 'im when I see 'im." Stone got out of the car. "I'll whistle and we break down both doors. All right?"

"All right." Hog climbed the steps to the front door. It was not particularly sturdy. It had four panels and two locks. He cocked the Uzi and waited.

When he heard Stone's whistle he drew back his foot and smashed it through one of the door panels, reached in and unlocked the door. No one came rushing toward him. He heard Stone and the Brit smash into the back door—then nothing.

Quietly, Hog crept into the front hall, the Uzi ready. No one. He heard Loughlin say: "Where the hell is everyone?"

Hog looked into the front bedroom. He poked the Uzi's muzzle into the closet. No one. Then he saw the wall. Someone had axed his way into the next apartment. There was a hole large enough to admit even him. Kneeling down, he peered through it into another bedroom.

Behind him he heard Stone say, "Son of a bitch!"

Hog said, "He's in the next county now, and still runnin'." He moved through the hole and stood up. The axe was lying by the empty bed. The room looked very bare, as if it were not being used. Stone and Loughlin followed him.

They searched the apartment quickly. There were two bodies in the kitchen. One was the slim man Neff had hired, the other an older woman, obviously the occupant of the apartment. They had each been shot several times. The back door was ajar. Apparently Neff had gone down the stairs after they came up. He was only minutes ahead of them.

"He had a car down there," Stone said in a disgusted tone. He turned to Loughlin. "Maybe you can find someone down there who saw him go. If we can get a line on his car..."

"Righto." Loughlin went down the stairs to the mews.

Stone telephoned Carol and reported what they had done and found. "Give us an hour before you mention it to the cops. We'll look for whatever we can find and get out. They won't like it but if they haul us in we might be in the slam for days."

"Yes," Carol said. "The police are barely civil to me now." She sighed. "Don't leave fingerprints."

"Right."

Stone hung up as Loughlin returned.

"There's a body in a car down there."

"What?" Stone jumped up. "Is it Neff?"

"No. I think it's Danzig. He matches the description. Pudgy little guy. Shot several times..."

"Holy shit," Hog said, "we's knee deep in bodies."

# Chapter Eighteen

Odile Buchon was astonished when Karl Neff showed up at her door, saying he would pay what he owed her. She asked him in. He paid—and stayed with her; he had managed to flee with a goodly amount of money. Money changed everything.

For Neff it was a good hideout. Odile had been set free by the police, who were no longer interested in her. Also the apartment had two doors, and an attic from which it was easily possible to get onto the roof.

Neff had thought at first to get out of Germany, for his life's sake. He knew von Schiller wanted him dead. But, weighing the risks against the gain—the possible gain—he decided to stay. For a time. There were things he knew that might cause money to flow his way. Blackmail could be lucrative.

Von Schiller had millions.

And happily for Neff, von Schiller was a suspected man because of his Nazi past. He had been more than a simple soldier doing his duty. He had been a killer of civilians, and a looter.

At the same time, von Schiller had political ambitions. The only thing important to him was power. He had power now, over the people he employed, but that was unsatisfactory—it was not enough. He had ideas of power that embraced nations. He was not a small thinker.

However, the Nazi hunters had evidence of his Nazi

past. It was not conclusive evidence; there were photographs of von Schiller in uniform, for instance, but that was to be expected. There were depositions by people who swore von Schiller had killed their parents or friends or relatives. Von Schiller could deny these, or prove he was elsewhere.

Karl Neff was aware of all this, had heard it discussed privately by von Schiller and some of his war cronies. They would all testify in his behalf—whatever he wanted them to say.

But there was one man who *did* have damaging evidence.

Anton Stael had been a high-placed clerk in the Hitler government. Thousands of documents of every description came across his desk. Some of them he copied and put away. Anton Stael was a man who thought about the future. He was one of those who had no faith at all in Hitler, but who never said so until after the war. Stael had many close Jewish friends who died in the concentration camps. He was of a mind to avenge them.

According to the documents he possessed, one of the men who sent them there was Rudolf von Schiller.

When he heard, through secret sources, that von Schiller was back in Germany, he sent von Schiller a note demanding a great sum of money to keep his silence. He accompanied the note with one of the damaging documents to prove his case.

Von Schiller tried to have him killed.

Anton Stael knew his man and expected that response. He had changed his name and took elaborate precautions so that von Schiller was never able to track him down.

Karl Neff had been part of that effort, had seen the document, and believed Stael had more like it. He suspected that Stael had blackmailed many former German officers, but von Schiller was the big game. Von Schiller should make him a million—or von Schiller would either kill him, or never come to power in Germany.

Anton Stael was willing to play that kind of game.

Karl Neff believed that with diligence and a little luck he could turn up Anton Stael. Then he would have von

Schiller in his power. He would allow von Schiller to rise as high as he could go—but always there would be money flowing into Neff's hands. A lot of money.

They sat in the brick-lined room with Carol and Hans Meydel, a gloomy meeting.

"We can slip into Osten," Stone said, "and see what we can stir up . . . but I think the chances are good we'll find nothing."

Loughlin nodded. "If Karl Neff is smart he'll be in Antarctica by now."

"Eatin' fish in an igloo," Hog put in. "We got no leads."

"Danzig is dead," Meydel said. "That closes off that avenue. Everyone who had anything to do with—"

"Wait a minute," Stone said, "not everyone!"

"What?"

"Odile Buchon. She was connected to that killing—to Karl Neff. Where is she now?" Stone snapped his fingers.

"Frankfurt," Hog said. "I remember those pictures of her in the paper."

Loughlin said, "I think we should find her."

"Could she be a lead?" Carol tapped a pencil against her chin.

"Who knows?" Stone said. "A lead is a lead is a lead, as what's-her-name said. We'll have to check it out. What else do we have?"

"As you say, Osten may be too tough a nut to crack. Someone has certainly taken Neff's place there—if he's gone for good."

A letter had arrived from the informant at Osten. Karl Neff had disappeared and no one had any ideas where, the informer wrote. Also, things were much more lax all of a sudden. A man named Dicot had been named head of the section. There seemed to be no plans going forward but there was gossip about capturing an American ambassador. So far it was only talk. And the informer thought there was confusion in the leadership.

He could not tell them why Neff was replaced by Dicot or why Neff had been in Berlin. There was some gossip about it, the informer wrote, but none of it made sense since no one knew any facts. The speculation was that he was on a super-secret mission. But it was only speculation. The informer added some speculation of his own: perhaps Neff had been casing an ambassador.

"What bothers me," Stone said, "is why Neff killed Danzig. Wasn't Danzig part of the organization?"

"Do you know positively that he killed Danzig?"

Loughlin said, "The body was still warm when I found it. He had been shot only minutes before, and Herr Neff was in the mews at that time."

"Well, why was Danzig sittin' in the mews?" Hog asked. "He'd been there a time, because his car engine was cold. Did he go there to shoot Neff?"

"That would explain a few things," Carol said. "The mysterious general hires Danzig to kill Neff, and instead Neff shoots Danzig. Also, that's why this man Dicot is head of the section at Osten. Because Neff is not going back there."

"I'll buy that," Loughlin said. "Bloody good."

"Okay, I like it too," Stone agreed. "That's why Neff has disappeared. They have drummed him out of the corps."

"But they ain't coiled his cable," Hog said. "What you're sayin' is that him and this here general is on the outs." He grinned at them. "We got us a little three-way goin' here."

Carol mused, "I wonder if Neff is alone—or has friends with him?"

"He prolly knows a lot of folks," Hog replied. "Somebody'll be on his side."

"Let's go check out Odile," Stone said.

"She doesn't know what we look like," Loughlin observed. "We could go right in the place . . ."

"If she's hookin' again, you could go in and have a little powwow," Hog said.

"We'll play it by ear." Stone got up.


Karl Neff rented a small sports car with a hard top. He wore a cap and went to have a look at the house von

Schiller lived in. The house was set back from a curving drive; it was in an exclusive section, with trees and shrubs hiding it from the street.

As he expected, the house was well guarded. There were two men sitting in a car on the street; the fence was high and might be electrified. He drove past at an even speed, puffing on a cigarette so that his face was hidden from the watchers. He would very much like to put a bullet or two into von Schiller, but reason dictated a better course. He would bleed the man.

But in order to do that, he would have to convince von Schiller he was in earnest. And this was a good time to start. Von Schiller was stubborn; it might take a while to convince him.

Neff parked the car and walked back in the gloom. It was after two in the morning and everything was silent. There were no lights on the street.

When he approached the car with the two guards, he crawled along the damp grass. They were both facing away from him, but if one turned, he could not see a crawling man . . . unless he leaned out of the car window.

Neff could hear voices as he got near. They were talking about a woman named Lisa. One of them was describing her unusual talents. Neff pulled Danzig's pistol, now equipped with a silencer, from his belt and stood up. He pushed the muzzle through the window, almost against the chest of the nearest man, and pulled the trigger twice. The second man yelped and reached for a gun and Neff shot him three times.

He glanced around, then reached in and felt for pulses. There were none.

He walked back to the rented car and drove away. That would cause von Schiller to squirm a bit.

Neff spent the rest of that day reviewing what he knew about Anton Stael. The man was probably in his late sixties by now, doubtless living in some respectable, settled community under a different name, maybe even with a wife. Very likely with a wife. She would be a good part of his camouflage.

Stael's hobby had been collecting clocks. Had he continued that? Why would he not? He was also a chess player. Maybe now he was meeting friends in a public park for a game now and then.

He had no photograph of Stael but he had a good description. He could assume the man lived in a good middle-class neighborhood and probably gave it out that he was retired. Neff studied a street map and decided on several areas, marking them carefully on the map.

# Chapter Nineteen

Carol's people had gotten Odile's address from the police and had given it to Stone and his men late that afternoon, and that evening they drove by the apartment where Odile Buchon was staying.

"If she's hooking again," Hog said, "she won't mind a few visitors."

Loughlin observed, "She spoke English on television. Who's going to speak to her?"

"You," Stone decided. "You look more European than we do."

"All right. What do I say?"

"Tell 'er she's got great tits," Hog said. "Always compliment a lady."

Stone sighed. "We're looking for Karl Neff. I don't know how you'll work that into the conversation, but you'll think of something."

"Righto." Loughlin made a face. "I'll think of something."

"I've seen her pictures," Hog said. "I could think of something. Maybe I better go up there."

"And offer her some of those goddamn grits?"

"Knock it off," Stone said. He pointed to Loughlin. "You go up the front steps. I'll be behind you and Hog goes around the back. Okay?"

"Righto. Five minutes to get into position?"

Hog waved and trotted away.

"If she's got a customer, just slide out," Stone said, "but tell 'er you'll be back . . . say in an hour." He looked at his watch. "It's almost twelve."

"I'll play it by ear." Loughlin opened the downstairs door and went in. He left his Uzi with Stone and mounted the stairs silently. At the top was a landing with two doors facing each other. Each door had a brass nameplate receptacle. One said: Roessler; the other: Buchon.

He glanced at Stone, fifteen feet below him, and rapped on the door. It took several minutes and a second rap before the door opened. Music spilled out and Odile Buchon, in a clinging pink wrap, smiled at him. *"Ja?"*

"Hello," he said in English. "Are you available?" And as he said the words, he saw Karl Neff. The man was in the next room, in the doorway, but reflected in a mirror several feet away. Possibly he did not know he'd been seen.

But Odile saw the look on Loughlin's face—he had not been able to hide the surprise.

Instantly she slammed the door and he heard the click of a bolt. He yelled to Stone, "It's Neff in there!"

He ran down the steps and Stone asked, "Did he see you?"

"Yes. And he's seen me before."

They went out into the street and Stone said, "He can't stay in there . . . he'd be bottled up. He doesn't know how many are after him. You stay here. I'll go around and warn Hog."

"Right."

Stone jogged around the building row, but Hog had not seen anyone come out. "Neff's in there?"

"Yes—and I'll bet he's getting away over the roofs." Stone ran to the end of the building row while Hog went in the other direction. They hadn't expected to find Neff there, and if he had climbed to the roof from Buchon's apartment, there were a hundred ways he might get down to the street level. They could hardly watch them all. He swore under his breath and jerked his head around, hearing shots.

Three shots, then two more, came from the far end of

the long building. Stone ran hard, arriving in time to see Loughlin reloading his pistol. "The bastard got away!"

"What happened?"

The Brit pointed. "He came down that lattice onto the top of the porch there, and jumped to the ground——"

"It was Neff?"

"Yes. Positive. I was too far away when I saw him climbing down the lattice. He ran to a car and jumped in—small sports car. I ran into the street and got off five shots but the car didn't swerve, so I guess I missed him. Too bad."

"Yes, too bad. Lousy light for good shooting." Stone glanced around. "We'd better haul out of here. Someone might have called the Polizei."

They collected Hog and drove back to tell Carol what they'd found. Carol was there, waiting for them.

She listened to the report, sipping a glass of red wine. At the end she looked disappointed. "So he got away..."

"Bloody clean," Loughlin said, making a face. "But we can pull the girl in for questioning. Put the screws on. She might know where he's gone."

"Probably a slight chance," Carol grumbled.

"Yeh. He's too smart to spread much around," Stone said.

"It must be a terrible life," Hog said, and they all stared at him.

Karl Neff was not hit by Loughlin's bullets. But there were five bullets in the little rented car, a minor concern compared to the fact that he had been located.

How had the Americans found him? Or was it luck? Maybe they had followed Odile and lucked onto him. That was probably it.

He telephoned Odile. The police had been to see her, but she had claimed Neff had only chanced to be there and that she knew nothing of his whereabouts. Probably they had not believed her, and had put a watch on her apartment.

"You mustn't come here again."

He thought it likely they had put a tap on her phone,

too. He told her to call him from a public telephone. "Call Fatty's number tonight—you remember Fatty?"

"Of course."

Fatty was a member of another underground group. He lived in a rabbit warren of apartments. His name was Julius but few called him that. He was glad to see Neff and poured out wine sitting on a kitchen table. Fatty was painfully thin, with sunken eyes and cheeks. He was an addict and completely undependable, except that he hated police.

"You need a place to stay? Stay here. You can have the bed."

"Thanks, Fatty, but I'll sleep on the floor. I don't mind."

"Are they after you?"

"Yes, but they don't worry me." They did not discuss who "they" were, but Neff was sure it meant police to Fatty.

He made a number of telephone calls from a public box and learned of the de Brunhoff gathering. The countess was nearly always good for a donation to right-wing activities. Her guest list was always restricted; he would not be able to get in, but it was a certainty, he thought, that von Schiller would be there. How could he hurt von Schiller short of killing him?

And short of having the material from Anton Stael to use.

He thought about it as he went about talking to watchmakers.


Neff located an old man who said he had become friendly with a clock collector named Jack Harris, a Britisher who spoke perfect German, and who was retired and lived quietly with his wife and a dog.

It sounded exactly like Stael.

But Neff said this was not the "brother" he was seeking. However, Neff said to the old man, "He may know my brother since they have the same hobby."

The old watchmaker could give him only an approximate address, and Neff went there at once and had the luck to meet a postman who gave him the correct address.

It was a modest house on a quiet street.

Could he possibly buy what Stael had. Stael had tried to blackmail von Schiller, and was probably still in the midst of prying money out of the general . . . so he would probably not sell. He would be a fool to sell.

So Neff would have to take it all by force.

He would go to the door and shoot Stael at once—if he had to. Stael was an old man, not a soldier. It should be simple.

But what if Stael did not keep the material in the house? He would have to keep Stael alive, to make sure. The wife might know nothing at all.

He drove by the house several times, looking it over carefully. There was nothing unusual about it. Stucco with wood paneling and a sturdy nail-studded gate, the house was between two others just like it. There was no sidewalk and all the windows were shuttered.

Well, he would have to do what he had to do.

That evening he drove to the area and parked the rented car a short distance away and walked to the house, recalling Stael's description. If the man was totally different . . .

The silenced pistol was just under his coat, easily at hand. He rapped hard on the door. He could hear nothing from inside the house. But in a moment the door opened and a thickset woman looked at him. *"Ja?"*

In that moment Neff saw the young man with the submachine gun cradled in his arms. He was standing across the darkened room, partially hidden by an ornate screen. "What is it?" the woman said.

Neff thought fast. This had to be Stael's house—and he was taking precautions. He said, "I'm looking for the home of Herr Eberling, please."

"You have the wrong house," the woman said, and shut the door.

Neff backed away and turned, taking a long breath. He had underestimated Anton Stael.

And now they had seen him.

# Chapter Twenty

Anton Stael was greatly alarmed. "What did he want, the man who came to the house?"

"He asked for someone else, Papa." Franz Stael made sure the door was securely bolted. He had seen the stranger's eyes on him and on the submachine gun, and he was very disturbed, but he did his best to conceal his feelings from his father. The old man was more excitable than he used to be, and it was not good for his heart.

"He looked like a salesman, Papa," Hanna Stael said. "Don't be upset."

Anton shook his head. "They have found me . . ."

"No, no, no, Papa," Franz led the old man to a chair and sat him down.

"We must move at once. Von Schiller is ruthless! He is capable of bombing the entire house! He will kill us all!"

Franz looked at his mother. She sighed and went to a cupboard and took down a bottle. Shaking two pills out, she got a glass of water. "It's time for your pills, Papa."

"Ach! Pills!" But he took them and gulped down the water.

"There is nothing here for them to find," Franz said. "They would be fools to think we would keep documents here."

Anton leaned back and closed his eyes. "You do not know them. You are too young. The Nazis were worse than devils, and von Schiller was the worst of all."

"But this is a different time, Papa."

Anton waved his hand. "Time . . . what do you think that means to von Schiller? He has not changed." He stared at his son. "We must go at once—to save our skins."

"If you are right, are they watching the house then?"

"Go and see. They will have to watch from a car."

"Is that wise?" Hanna asked.

Franz smiled. "I will be a shadow in the night. They will not even see me. I will go out the back and give a whistle when I return." He pulled on a dark sweater.

Anton rose. "Let us put some things into the van."

Franz made a circle of the streets and there were no parked vehicles where the house could be watched. No one was on the street, not in any of the doorways. Was his father right? The old man had been right so many times. . . . His fear of von Schiller was very real, and for a very good reason. The documents could bury von Schiller.

Franz returned. "The way is clear now."

"Then let us go. Franz, you drive. I will open the gate."


Neff could feel it in his bones. He had been so close to Anton Stael; the man must have been in the next room.

But who was that with the submachine gun? Maybe his son.

So there were probably three of them in the house. He had not known Stael had a son. And if the son was in on the blackmail, he was one more to account for. The son could take up where the father left off. Not good.

But there was an urgency to the business now. They had seen him; they would probably suspect something was in the wind. After all, Stael had been hiding from von Schiller for many years. It must have done something to his psyche by now. He might be full of what the doctors were calling stress.

And because of it he might make stupid mistakes.

How could he get them out of the house, into the open?

What about fire? Molotov cocktails? A few thrown against the house and it would be a flaming pyre in moments.

Would Stael keep the documents in the house? He might. And if he did, he would certainly save them first.

Neff would be nearby. He would gun down the lot of them and be off with the documents.

It sounded almost too easy. The son might fire back—but he would be ready for that.

He had to try it. Von Schiller probably had men looking for him this minute. Time could be running short. But when he got his hands on the documents, time would mean nothing. Then he would turn the screws and von Schiller would pay. . . .

He forced himself to be cautious. He drove past the house at odd times but could see no activity, nothing unusual. The house was apparently shut up. Naturally, a man like Anton Stael would not gossip with neighbors.

It was possible to park the rented car a good distance away and keep some sort of watch on the house with binoculars. But while he watched, no one went in or came out.

The night was overcast and cool but did not feel like rain. He waited till very late, till all the house lights along the street were out. He stopped the car across from the Stael house and, leaving the engine running, stepped out and quickly lighted three of the Molotov cocktails.

With a last look around, the Uzi close at hand, he threw them at the house, one after the other.

The glass bottles smashed; the petrol ignited instantly in large splashes and began to eat at the wood. The fire blazed up in a red-orange pyre, beginning to crackle at once. In moments the house seemed engulfed in flame.

But no one came running out.

As the fire grew in strength, lighting up the entire street, lights began to come on in neighboring houses and several people shouted, "Fire!"

Neff got back in the car, astonished that the house was apparently empty. Had they gone out the back way? But it would be natural to run into the street! There was no alley behind the house. . . .

Someone yelled at him. He put the car in gear and moved away fast. No one had been home! The realization came hard. After his visit they had all moved out! No wonder the house had seemed shut up. It was!

He swore, growling the words as he sped away. Now he would have to do it all over again.

"The police would dearly love to arrest von Schiller," Carol Jenner said, "but they need more evidence of crimes. He is accused of all sorts of things during the Hitler years, and the Nazi Hunters are pressing the case, but so far . . ." She shrugged. "In my talks with the police they tell me that evidence is lacking and they may not be able to convict if they put him on trial."

"So they're slow to move?"

"Yes. And we cannot be positive he is behind Karl Neff."

"Your informant thought so," Stone said.

Carol nodded. "And I think so too." She shrugged. "But proof is difficult. And von Schiller is only one of a group of ex-Nazis who may all be working with him. It gets complicated."

"Any news of Neff?" Loughlin asked.

"We've got listeners out everywhere," Carol said, "snoops and spies and informers, but no one has turned him up. We heard an interesting bit of information, though. Two of von Schiller's private guards were murdered."

"Where was this?"

"Outside von Schiller's estate. They were sitting in a car and someone shot them both."

"Damn! That will make it harder for us to get into his house." Mark Stone scowled. "Who did it? Neff?"

"Maybe. No one knows, of course. If our theory is right that von Schiller tried to have Neff killed—using Danzig—then Neff may be getting back at von Schiller any way he can. It would be like him."

"He's bloody cold-blooded," Loughlin observed.

Carlo Vanner was unable to identify the person who had exposed von Schiller to the Nazi Hunters. It was probably someone, he told von Schiller, who had no connection with the Hunters and had called or written them one time. And it was possible the Nazi Hunters did not know the identity of the informer.

Von Schiller had to agree.

But he had received another copy of a most damaging document from Anton Stael, demanding a large sum of money or the paper would be turned over to the proper authorities.

It could not be ignored.

"Make a partial payment," Vanner urged. "Tell him that you cannot pay it all—give him some plausible excuse— stall for time. I will do my best to root him out."

Grumpily, von Schiller nodded. The money was sent with a carefully written letter, with no signature, to a town outside Frankfurt, addressed to a post office box. Carlo sent a man to watch the box, but no one came to pick up the letter.

However, another letter arrived from Stael complaining that the payment was not sufficient.

Von Schiller raved and screamed, pounding a table— but in final he sent more money. He knew he had only bought a bit of time. The sword above his head was still there. His ambitions were of necessity put on hold until Stael could be found and eliminated.

Carol Jenner's anonymous informer reported that nothing was going forward at Osten. No plans were being made or discussed. It was as if the organization were being gradually dismantled.

And the informant had no reason for it—except rumors. It was said that the head of the organization was devoting all his time to one project. No one knew what it was.

The informant knew nothing about von Schiller.

Stone, Hog and Loughlin made themselves familiar with the area around von Schiller's big house. There were trees and shrubs aplenty to conceal watchers. There was little traffic in and out of the house, a few tradesmen delivering necessities, and now and then a repairman, but little else.

However one particular car, an old-model Mercedes, went in and out every day with two men inside.

Loughlin borrowed a motorcycle from the motor pool and was able to tail the car. He reported it made a dozen stops and the men got out and talked to various people. It seemed to him the two were looking for someone. Without much luck.

The two men also visited a burned-out house and talked to neighbors. Loughlin jotted down the address and Carol Jenner requested information about the house. She learned it had been set afire by Molotov cocktails thrown by a person or persons unknown. The house was occupied by a Britisher, Jack Harris, and his family, who had not been hurt in the fire and had disappeared without a trace.

Several things were suspicious, Carol said to them. "First, the method of starting the fire sounds like someone from the military might have thought of it; second, the family has disappeared; and third, why was von Schiller so interested in it?"

Meydel asked, "D'you think von Schiller started the fire?"

"Probably not—or he wouldn't send men to ask the neighbors about it," Stone said.

Loughlin said, "Well, he might be asking if they survived. Or if one particular person survived. We ought to find out what they're asking."

"Yes. *Why* he's interested may be damned important—to us."

"So let's do 'er," Hog suggested.


The house in question was not totally destroyed, they saw when they arrived on the scene. The firemen had been efficient and had managed to save about half of it. The two adjoining homes had also been badly damaged and workmen were assessing it. An insurance firm was paying them, Loughlin learned by talking to a foreman.

Neighbors told Loughlin they had already talked to the police, but he wheedled out of them that the fire had started late at night; the family had not been seen in the house for several days before the fire. The Harris family had been very quiet and had kept to themselves for the most part. The old man, Jack Harris, had seemed more German than British, they said. He had taken daily walks, accompanied mostly by a small dog.

Three people had lived in the house: the older man and his wife and a grown son. The man was retired, but the neighbors did not know from what. The only thing they knew was that he collected clocks.

One neighbor said he had seen a small sports car in front of the house at the time of the fire and had shouted at the man inside, but the car had driven away fast. It was his opinion that that man had started the fire.

Another neighbor told Loughlin that he had seen the family van drive away from the house late at night, three days before the fire. He had been up, taking a pill, and had noticed the headlights.

Carol said, "That must have been when the family got out. Maybe they had a warning."

"A warning about what?"

Meydel said, "A warning they would be burned out."

"Then they should have gone to the police."

"Yes," Stone said, nodding. "Why didn't they? If they were warned, why did they just up and take off? What do they have to hide?" He smiled at them. "There's more here than meets the eye."

Carol said, "I'll talk to the British embassy and see what I can find out about Harris. Maybe there's something in his background that won't stand inspection."

"Good show," Loughlin agreed. "This Harris may be a key to something."

There was no Jack Harris in any records. The burned-out house had been in his wife's maiden name, Behn. Carol put two men digging into marriage records and discovered that Hanna Behn had married Anton Stael in 1941, in Berlin.

Was Anton Stael calling himself Jack Harris? If so, why?

It took very little digging to find that Anton Stael had been a high-placed clerk in the Hitler government for three years. At the war's end he had gone back to civilian life in Frankfurt as an accountant, and there the record ended. Presumably he had changed his name to Harris for unknown reasons and dropped out of sight. He and his family had lived in the house only a year and a half.

"It gets curiouser and curiouser," said Stone. "There is something fishy about Anton Stael."

Carol asked, "Could he have known von Schiller during the war?"

Loughlin shook his head. "Not bloody likely. Von Schiller was a general and Stael a clerk. They wouldn't mix."

They frowned at each other. Carol said, "Doesn't there *have* to be some kind of connection? Why did von Schiller send two men to ask questions? Isn't he trying to find Anton Stael?"

"We simply don't know enough," Hans Meydel said. "None of what we know adds up to anything usable. There's something else. Maybe von Schiller and Stael are blood relations."

"Cousins?" Hog asked. "Maybe Stael did Schiller's income tax and the government's after him."

"Wait a minute," Stone said. "Records. Stael dealt with records during the war." He shook his head. "But why would von Schiller want war records at this late date?"

"Remember what Carol said about war crimes?" Loughlin ventured. "The records are probably detrimental to von Schiller. He wants to burn them."

"But why didn't they come out years ago?"

Loughlin smiled. "I'm just posing the questions. *You* figure the answers. What if the records were lost and Stael has copies?"

Stone said, "That's an idea. It would account for what's happened."

"And why Stael has disappeared." Carol snapped her fingers. "He's afraid for his life."

"I like it," Stone said. "It has character." He sighed. "Of course, we may all be out in left field. It could be something else altogether.

"Like what?" Hog asked. "Ever'body try to think of some other reason that's as good."

There was silence.

# Chapter Twenty-one

Stone said, "If Anton Stael has evidence that would cook von Schiller, then he's on our side. We ought to find him and help him."

"Jolly good thought," Loughlin agreed. "How do we find him?"

"He's probably been hiding out for years," Carol mused. "He's probably had a dozen different names. It might be impossible to trace him."

"Well, we know a few things about him. He's a clock collector, for one," Loughlin said. "But I suppose he's given that up for the time being. He'd be smart to."

"We'd better concentrate on Neff and von Schiller," Stone said definitely. "Stael will be too difficult to turn up. At least we know where von Schiller is. Let's try to learn more about him . . . and his plans."

Anton Stael was too elusive, but his demands were not excessive and von Schiller was advised to pay. He shouted and raved and screamed at them, but finally he paid. It was the best course for the moment. They would keep men at it, attempting to locate Stael—and if they did, the picture would change; but for now, he was advised to pay. He could easily afford it.

There was another advantage to paying the blackmail, his advisors said: Then they could go on with their plans . . . which were several. The organization dealt in drugs and black-market weapons, and these had not been affected; business as usual prevailed.

But the kidnapping of an American official for ransom had stalled.

The appointment of a new American secretary of state had been announced, but the new secretary had no plans to visit Europe in the near future.

The elimination of a high-ranking British official, Sir George Cummings, was in the works. Cummings was in the forefront of Britain's efforts to control terrorists. A conference had been called, to be held in Brussels to that end, and international VIPs would attend.

If Sir George were done away with, it would send the entire conference into confusion.

Carol Jenner's no-name informant at Osten called her on the telephone. He was allowed much free time of late, he told her; things were very lax. But there were insistent rumors of big things in the offing and he feared that discipline would soon tighten and he would be unable to get word to her easily. He outlined a plan whereby he would be able to place notes to her in a particular spot by a road leading to the estate. She could have someone slip in at night to pick them up.

He had heard nothing of Karl Neff.

Von Schiller approved the program concerning Sir George Cummings. It would take some heat off them in Germany. He sent one of his old army comrades to deal with the matter. Heribert Muller, an ex–general officer, was entrusted with the task. He had been a staff officer on von Schiller's staff and was considered a brain.

He was a stout gray man approaching seventy, vigorous and demanding. He had become wealthy along with von Schiller and was very fond of women; almost any woman who was attractive caught his roving eye. His wife knew of his philandering but closed her mind to it and busied herself with her garden. They had been sleeping in separate bedrooms for more than thirty years.

Muller picked several men to accompany him and left for Brussels at once.

Carol's informant learned of the move when his woman friend told him; her husband was one of the men. General Muller, Uto Schrenck, Georg Werfel and her husband, Walter Rekowski, had gone on a super-secret mission. Her husband, she told the informant, was well known as an expert marksman and he had told her he thought it was for this reason he had been chosen.

Carol called a meeting at once, reporting the note she had received. The informant could not tell her why the men had gone to Brussels . . . but if Muller had gone it must be important.

"What is taking place in Brussels?"

"The Conference on Terrorists is about to be held—will that do?" Meydel grinned at them. "It's been in the newspapers. I would say that Muller has gone to assassinate one of the members." Meydel had a sheet of paper, and read from it. "Here is a list of von Schiller's staff men during the war. Heribert Muller was one of them. There are five in all, high-ranking men. Three are dead, one is in a hospital in Bavaria, and Muller is on his way to Belgium."

"So we alert the Belgian cops," Stone said approvingly.

"We must," Carol said. "Of course, we have no idea who the target or targets might be."

"At least they will be able to keep Muller and his crew under surveillance."

Loughlin asked, "How many members to the conference?"

"Probably fifty or sixty," Carol replied. "Not including aides and other staff."

"A bloody regiment!"

"And probably Muller will blend right in," Stone observed. "He'll have documents and papers, of course, to gain entry anywhere he wishes. And he knows who he's after."

Loughlin said, "How many would he have to kill to break up the conference?"

"Not many," Carol said, shaking her head. "I suppose any one of the leaders would shake them up. I'm sure the Belgians will think of that . . . but we'll remind them."

"I'll take care of it," Hans Meydel said. He gathered up his papers and went out.

Hog spoke up. "Well, are we goin' too?"

They looked at each other. Carol said, "Sleep on it. What would we gain? What would we lose here? The Belgian police would resent you. . . . I know that hasn't bothered you in Frankfurt and Berlin—"

They went back to their rooms and discussed it among themselves. What would they gain? The Belgian police were probably very competent at surveillance; what could they add to it?

They decided in the end that it might be foolish to go and lose what advances they had made here. They were keeping close scrutiny on von Schiller and were bound to turn up Karl Neff. He had given them the slip one time too many.

Loughlin on his motorcycle again tailed the two men in the old Mercedes. The others, by questioning some of those questioned by the two men, had learned their names. They were Carlo Vanner and Ludwig Krone. Carlo was obviously the leader. And Carlo was looking for a man named Anton Stael who collected clocks and liked to play chess. Why he was looking for Stael was not divulged.

"We could easy collect them two," Hog said, "and take them outa circulation."

"Von Schiller would only send out more." Stone looked at photos of von Schiller's house. "Is it possible to get inside, d'you think?"

"What for?"

"To plant a listening device or two."

"We could try," Loughlin said, "but they probably sweep it daily, looking for bugs."

Stone sighed deeply. "Yeah . . ."

The Brussels police duly filed the information and warnings from Germany. The information was not specific; it did not name a particular possible target. It only asked that General Muller be placed under surveillance.

But the police force was spread thin during the conference and there were not enough men to take care of all such foreign warnings. Spot checks were made on Muller and the reports did not show suspicious activity on his part. The spot checks became fewer.

Georg Werfel and Uto Schrenck obtained a room in the same hotel with Sir George Cummings, the British target. The two Germans had papers from the media in their own country—as did hundreds of others. Walter Rekowski occupied a room in General Muller's suite, as his valet.

Werfel and Schrenck followed Sir George everywhere for several days, noting his every movement, till they could almost predict his actions. He was a creature of habit. Every afternoon he met with half a dozen others in an exclusive coffeehouse. He went there by taxi and could be depended upon to come out of the hotel the same time every day. The doorman would hail him a cab.

"It's the best chance to get him," Werfel told Muller. "A shot from a car on the opposite side of the street. No one will know where the shot came from. The car will move away—"

"Excellent," Muller said, pulling at his mustache. "Splendid. Rent a car in the morning. Walter, you have the rifle?"

"Yes, General."

"Very good. One of you will drive the car. Walter will shoot from the back." He looked at them. "Yes?"

They nodded, and Werfel smiled. "We will drive to the marshes and lose the rifle, then return the car."

General Muller was pleased. "I will be in the restaurant with a dozen others at that time." He tapped Walter's chest. "Tomorrow then."

"Yes, General."

"You both know Sir George by sight? No mistakes."

"Yes, General. We know him very well."

"Good."

Werfel was right. It went like clockwork. They rented a dark BMW, a four-door. In the back seat Walter Rekowski could lay the rifle along the top of the front seat and fire through the open window. One shot was all he would need, he said.

Uto went along; he sat beside Walter to roll down the

window at the right moment. Werfel drove the car.

Sir George Cummings came out of the hotel as he always did; he was wearing a tan overcoat and a dark homburg and carried a cane that he tapped on the sidewalk as he spoke to the doorman. The doorman ran to the street, whistling for a cab. Werfel drove along the opposite side of the street and halted the car as Walter said, "Now."

The shot cracked sharp inside the car. A quick glance showed Werfel that Sir George was hit; the man crumpled to the pavement, his cane flying. All around him, people rushed to assist him, not realizing what had happened.

Werfel moved the car away smoothly as Uto rolled up the window again.

"Not too fast, not too fast," Uto said in a tight voice. "Get the gun out of sight, Walter"

They were a block away before Werfel said, "Good shot, Walter."

"Right through the heart," Uto agreed. He looked back. "They don't know yet what happened."

Walter nodded, busy breaking down the rifle; he put it into the heavy cloth bag and zipped it up.

Werfel threaded his way out of town skillfully and they drove steadily for an hour on an arrow-straight road, listening to the reports of the incident on the car radio. Sir George was dead and there was a terrible commotion at the hotel with police everywhere. An on-the-spot reporter was excited; the background was filled with whistles and shouts. . . .

"I am saddened to report that Sir George Cummings has been shot dead. At the moment the police have no leads but they expect an arrest to be made before nightfall."

Werfel laughed. "They've got no idea at all! They're probably searching the buildings on the opposite side of the street!"

"Yes, someone may have fired from a window," Uto chuckled. "Maybe no one saw us at all."

They reached the marshes, a dank, smelly area. Birds, startled by the car on the lonely road, rose into the air and circled. Werfel drove along several miles to be sure no one else was about. Then he stopped the car and Walter got out with the cloth bag. He walked down through the fringe of cattails to a dense spot and heaved the bag as far out as he could.

It sank instantly into the oily depths with hardly a splash.

He got back in the car. "No one will ever find that."

Werfel backed the car around and they went back. He was in a very good mood. It had all gone off beautifully. "What a place to drop your mother-in-law," he said, and they laughed. Too bad they hadn't brought along a bottle, to celebrate a little.

General Muller was delighted with them when they returned. They went up to his suite one by one, taking care that no one saw them enter. Muller went to the bar and poured drinks all around. He had been listening to the radio, he told them. "The police are totally confused. They have no idea where the shot came from. Apparently no one heard it—because of the traffic noises." He wrung Walter's hand. "I congratulate you on a perfect operation."

"Thank you, sir."

"Now drink up and hurry along," he said to Werfel and Uto. "We must never be seen together at any time. I assume you will be going home immediately..."

"In a few days, General."

"Very good." Muller shook hands with them and saw them out.

When the two had gone, he said to Rekowski, "I am very pleased with you, Walter. Of course you got rid of the gun?"

"Yes, certainly, General. And thank you, sir."

"Fine." Muller clasped his hands together.

The police did not bother to interview General Muller. Half a hundred people, including many Belgian officials, had seen him in the hotel restaurant at the time of the shooting. Muller had given a luncheon and several prominent Belgians were guests of honor.

The conference was shattered by the death of Sir George and never got back to business with any spirit. Many of the members left early.

# Chapter Twenty-two

The news of Sir George Cummings's death in Brussels was a blow to all in the Operations building. The terrorists had stolen a march on them. General Muller had succeeded in spite of the warnings given the police.

The Belgian police had been given the names of three men who were said to be working with General Muller, and these were checked out. Two were apparently journalists; the third was Muller's valet. It was said that the valet was an expert marksman, but was in no way criminal. Many people were marksmen.

The valet, Walter Rekowski, had stated he was in the restaurant with the general all afternoon and no one could say that he was not. The general said he was. When the police questioned those in the restaurant no one could remember seeing Rekowski, but then, no one had looked for him.

The British authorities were very angry about the way the affair was handled. But the general and his valet had departed the city and it was believed they had taken an airliner headed for Athens, Greece. Their departure had been very abrupt. Even Werfel and Schrenck had not been told they were going.

Sir George's remains were put on another plane and shipped to London for burial.

Von Schiller's house was under constant surveillance, and the watchers reported that a small party was given at the big house shortly after the death of the Britisher. It was assumed to be a celebration of the Brussels affair.

Automobile license numbers were taken down and compared with those taken at the de Brunhoff party. Many proved to be the same. Von Schiller's cronies and aides had assembled.

Stone and the others watched from a distance. Because of the elaborate detection devices around the house they were unable to come near. Quite probably plans were being discussed. . . .

Unfortunately, the police said, nothing of importance could be proved against von Schiller. The police and the Nazi Hunters did not want to bring him to trial until definite evidence would convict him without question. Carol's superiors had caused appeals to be broadcast urging Anton Stael to come forward, but he had not.

Then Carol's informant at Osten reported that his woman friend was very concerned. Her husband, Walter Rekowski, had not returned from Belgium. Uto and Georg Werfel had come back and had said they believed Walter had gone with General Muller to Greece.

But Muller's secretary had told Frau Rekowski, when she called, that Walter had not gone on holiday with the general . . . who was still in Greece. The secretary was in almost daily communication with the general, and he stated that Rekowski had gone back to Germany. "The general is surprised at the question," the secretary told Frau Rekowski. "He can tell you nothing more."

The informant reported that his woman friend did not believe Muller, but there was nothing she could do about it. She was afraid that if she became too insistent she herself might disappear.

Carol Jenner said, "It's one more case of 'The man who pulls the trigger is dead himself.'"

"They're a bloody group," commented Loughlin.

"Their system is correct in one thing," Stone said. "The dead do not testify worth a damn. Apparently Muller did this job himself . . . or had it done in Athens."

"There were two others in on this killing," Loughlin said. "I wonder how they feel about the shooter's disappearance. They are probably as guilty as he."

"They can't shoot ever'body in Germ  y," Hog observed. He frowned. "Or can they?"

"I think they would—to protect themselves," Stone said. "What do a few deaths mean to those goddamn Nazis?"

Neff's efforts to locate Anton Stael came to one dead end after another. It was as if the man had dropped into a hole. He was forced into a decision. If he could not use Stael's documents to ruin von Schiller, he would do it another way.

He would kill him. But even as he made that decision, his German sense of thoroughness pushed him into completing the work he had set out to do, area by area.

And in the very last area he came upon a watchmaker's shop and a man who also dealt in antiques. No, the watchmaker said, he did not know a clock collector, but he had recently bought a number of valuable antique clocks from a man who came in off the street.

His description of the man tallied with that of Anton Stael. The name the man had given meant nothing—Stael would use any name he happened to think of.

"This may be the man I'm looking for," Neff said. "Where does he live?"

"Why don't you know his name?" the watchmaker asked.

"Because he *is* a collector, and you know how secretive they are. I'm sure the name he gave you is not his right one."

"Well, I do know where he lives. He mentioned once that he lived not far away." The watchmaker gave Neff the address of a nearby apartment house.

Neff thanked the man and went out.

It was time to enlist another man or two because the apartment building had several entrances and exits. It would be impossible for one man to keep tabs on all.

He had it in mind to kidnap Anton Stael.

Vanner requested a meeting with General von Schiller and, when it was granted, faced the man in the general's office.

"Yes, what is it, Carlo?"

"I have to tell you, sir, this house is under surveillance."

"*Gott!* By the police?"

"I don't think so. One of my men says he thinks they are foreigners. He heard them speak in English."

Von Schiller got up and crossed the room, frowning. He opened a humidor and took out a cigar. "When did he hear this?"

"Last night, General. The man is an ex-forester and moves like a fox. One of them nearly stepped on him."

"I see." Von Schiller lit the cigar and puffed for a moment. "And what do you think, Carlo?"

"There are several possibilities. . . . The one that worries me the most is an assassination attempt on your life."

Von Schiller paused, staring at him. "Assassination!?"

"Certainly. Why else are they watching the house?"

"You don't know how long they have been there?"

Carlo shook his head. "No, sir."

"Hmmm. Why do I think instantly of Karl Neff? But you said they spoke English."

"He is one of the possibilities."

Von Schiller paced the room and came back, puffing the cigar. "What do you suggest, Carlo?"

"A change of scenery, sir."

The general shook his head shortly. "That would be most inconvenient at this time. Can't you deal with them?"

"Yes, sir. Of course, it will draw the attention of the police."

The older man shrugged. "It cannot be helped. I must defend myself against assassination."

Carlo nodded.

He had five men on guard duty at all times outside the big house. The ex-forester, Wolfgang, had detected the foreigners on the south side of the house; he could not say how many there were. But it took very few to watch.

Carlo told Wolfgang: "I think they're the three Americans we were after. And if they are, we must be very careful and lay our plans exactly."

"You think they are dangerous?"

Carlo grunted. "They are the most dangerous you will ever face."

Watching von Schiller's house was boring work. Loughlin, on the bike, followed the old Mercedes whenever it went out. Stone and Hog stayed at the house with binoculars, examining everything that happened, which wasn't much.

Stone and Hog split the watch.

Hog said, "They just brought three men, maybe four, an hour ago."

Stone frowned at the distant house. "I don't like it."

Hog pulled at his chin. "Well, if somethin's up, then let's figger it in military terms."

Stone grunted. "More men could mean an attack. Probably on us."

The big Texan grinned. "The odds is only six or eight t'one. Not bad."

Stone shook his head. "No sense in fighting at all. We'd better pull out. There's nothing at all we could gain by a fight here."

"Except knock some of them down."

"Not good enough." Stone looked at his watch, then glanced at the sky. "Be dark in an hour. What d'you think?"

"Well, best thing is to change position soon's it gets dark. It could be they got us spotted. Why don't we try t'see what they're up to?"

"Because there could be ten or more of them. Lots of firepower." He indicated the brush. "Nothing much to get behind."

Hog made a face and shrugged again. He gathered up his gear and slung the Uzi over his shoulder. "I'm ready when you-all are."

They waited till dark, then crept along a line of trees with tall grass and plants between them and the big house. To their left was the dirt road, and beyond it was a weedy ravine with a sandy bottom.

The first shots came from there, cutting the tops of the weeds just above their ears.

# Chapter Twenty-three

Instantly Stone flattened. To his right was a wide field lying fallow. He snaked his way to the right, ending up in a deep furrow. Glancing back, he saw Hog behind him; they could not be seen from the house.

Hog said, "They was fixin' to get behind us."

"Yes. Somebody fired too soon."

"Nervous," Hog replied.

They were reasonably safe from attack from the right. The enemy would be foolish to run across the open field into Uzi fire. The ground ahead of them looked jumbled and covered with brush. He motioned to Hog and crept that way.

Someone fired into the grass behind them, spraying the area.

Hog growled, "Wish to hell I had me some grenades."

Stone reached the jumbled area; as far as he could see from a prone position, it ran along the edge of the field. It looked like a plow had piled up the dirt in ridges and grass had overgrown it with tall weeds and brush.

He glanced at the western sky; it was getting darker. A mass of leaden clouds had obscured the sun but it did not feel like rain. He crawled into the brush, toward the ravine, taking enormous care not to give away his position. Hog was at his elbow, watching both flanks.

Stone found a spot where he could see the ravine, perhaps twenty feet of it, most in shadow. Three heads rose up as he looked, each one peering toward the line of trees. One of them gave an order and they started forward. One lifted a submachine gun and fired several bursts at a spot about five feet to the left of Stone.

Hog said, "That's too goddamn close."

Stone shoved his Uzi forward and the motion attracted one of the three men opposite. As he swung his weapon and yelled, Stone fired. The three disappeared.

It was silent. Then Hog asked, "You do any good?"

"Three," Stone said. He backed down again. "Let's get out of here." He motioned, and Hog crawled away quickly, cradling his Uzi.

They came to the end of the piled earth and Stone said, "Let's get into the ditch there."

"Right."

Someone was shouting a long way off; they could not hear what he was yelling. A car's engine roared as they halted under the line of trees, and a car sped along the road to stop several hundred yards away, in a grove.

"They're goin' to circle us," Hog said, glancing at the sky. "I figger they started too late." He grinned at Stone. "They're goin' to circle shit."

"Get moving." Stone slithered into the ravine, which was choked with brush. An automatic rifle stuttered somewhere along the line of trees some distance away.

Hog said, "They don't know where we are. Maybe they'll shoot each other."

Stone led away from the big house, moving slowly to make no sound. Just ahead someone kicked a rock and he hugged the ground, looking back at Hog. Hog nodded and moved left noiselessly, putting eight or ten feet between them. Then Hog tossed a rock to his left. It crashed in the brush and instantly two automatic weapons opened up on it.

Both Hog and Stone fired at the sounds, hearing a yelp, then silence.

They moved forward again and in a minute Stone came upon a body facedown in the weeds. Hog appeared from the left and whispered, "They's another one here." He pointed into a clump, then raised his head.

As he did so a burst of fire cut the brush beside him. Hog rolled. Stone rose and fired directly into the body of a man who stood almost above them. The bullets cut him in two, smashing him into a red ruin. Instantly Hog was on his knees searching the brush—but found no target. Some-one fired a single shot behind them that might have been a signal.

Stone said, "Come on." He got to his feet and jogged forward. In a moment he came to the car in the clump of trees. There was no one near it. He motioned to Hog. "Get this thing started."

Stone faced about with the Uzi as Hog slid under the wheel. The engine caught and Stone ran around and jumped in as Hog put the car in gear.

Half a dozen shots followed them down the road, then they were out of range. The car was a small Toyota, well battered, but it ran like a jackrabbit. Stone looked at the other. "They had that planned."

"Yeh, I reckon."

"You gonna turn the lights on?" Stone asked.

Hog switched them on.

They were on a side road that turned into a paved ave-nue. They had gotten clean away, and Stone doubted there would be a pursuit. Von Schiller would not want shooting in the streets of the city. Not a car chase, at any rate.

They drove back to discuss the affair with Carol. Loughlin had come in an hour before with nothing to re-port.

"They got their dander up," Stone said, "and apparently decided to cash in our chips."

"I wonder if it means anything," Carol mused.

Hans Meydel had just entered; he stared at Stone. "What's dander?"

Stone looked blank. Carol replied for him. "It's slang. 'Got their dander up' means they got angry."

"Ahhh. I think I know what cash in the chips means. They tried to kill you."

"They sure did," Hog said, nodding. "But bullets just bounce offen us."

Meydel eyed him. Meydel was not always sure about Hog.

Neff enlisted Fatty to help watch the apartment house. Fatty was good for nothing else, of course. He drilled the reedy little man in descriptions and placed him near one entrance, taking up his own position near the one more likely to be used.

Anton Stael did not take daily walks any longer. If he came out of the apartment, Neff did not see him. It was impossible to watch the door of the apartment too much without arousing the suspicions or curiosity of other tenants. If Stael's son went in and out, Neff could not tell.

At the end of the first day Fatty was worn out and disgusted. He had never staked out a house before and swore he never would again. He had seen no one who resembled Neff's descriptions, and he was tired of the whole thing. He demanded to be paid off, and when he got his money he waved and disappeared.

More and more Neff was convinced he would have to go into the apartment with a gun. If he waited too long the family might move again, in the dead of night. He would have to chance it.

When he went into the house he might have to use the pistol, and the noise would attract other residents. Someone was bound to call the police. He would have to be quick and he would have to have his retreat planned.

He parked his car in the closest spot and went in the nearest apartment entrance. Stael's apartment was on the second floor, number eleven.

He could hear radios or television sets in most apartments as he went up the stairs. The hallway smelled of cooked food. A man came out of a door farther along and passed Neff with a nod. He went down the steps and Neff heard the outer door open and close.

When he put his ear to the door of number eleven, there was no sound.

He pressed the grip of the pistol under his coat. He looked along the empty hallway and rapped on the door hard. There was no response. He rapped again.

A man's voice from inside said, "What is it?"

"Police!" Neff barked. "Open the door."

He thought he could hear someone scuttling . . . a chair fell over. Then silence.

Neff put his shoulder to the door—but it held. He stepped back and hit the door just above the lock with the heel of his boot, as hard as he could. The door sagged open and he ran in, the pistol poking this way and that.

No one was in the apartment.

A window was open. Neff flung the curtains aside and looked down. A man—it looked like Stael—was just jumping off a fire escape into a mews. The man ran into the night and disappeared.

Neff climbed out and followed. He was only half a minute behind! He flung himself off the escape and ran in the direction taken by Stael. He could not afford to let the man get away! Stael had been wearing a light-colored sweater —it should be easy to spot in the early dark.

He was in a narrow cement-floored parking area with few lights. Three men were talking and smoking to his right as he ran down the center. He yelled at them, "Did a man just run by?"

They pointed. Neff said, "Thanks," and continued. The apartments loomed over him on both sides and there were automobiles parked in neat rows. He turned a corner and could see no one in front of him. Had Stael turned in to one of the many doors? But none had been open or were swinging as he passed.

Neff turned another corner and there was an open space. He came to a metal fence that lined a deep cement storm drain. The fence was chest high and there was no one in the drain, twenty feet down.

But farther along, maybe a hundred feet, a man was trying to get over the fence.

Neff yelled, "Stop!" and ran toward the man. It was Stael.

The other stared at him for a moment, got his legs over the fence and suddenly let go.

Neff saw him fall, and hit hard on the pale cement. He hit and did not move. Neff ran to the spot above and looked down at the sprawled figure, shapeless in the dusk.

Neff looked both ways but there was no way down. It was too far to jump. Neff swore and pounded his fists on the fence. Stael had gotten away from him again.

The body was not discovered until morning. The police were called and an ambulance took the body away. Anton Stael was dead of multiple injuries.

The police could find no relatives to notify.

# Chapter Twenty-four

Carol said, "We've been able to get a report from German intelligence. We scratched their backs and they came across with a little something about von Schiller."

"Good or bad for him?" Stone asked.

"Not good, for us. The report says that all—or nearly all—terrorist groups are consolidating under von Schiller. That's probably what all those meetings at his house were about."

Loughlin remarked, "So we can expect stepped-up activity from them?"

"Probably." She had a small stack of photos and handed them around. "These were taken yesterday from a chopper that made one pass over the house. It looks like they've beefed up the security."

Stone frowned over the pictures. It did indeed. Shrubbery had been chopped down, a few trees taken out . . . it would be difficult to get within several hundred yards of the house without being spotted. And the photos did not show the patrols or guards that were bound to be posted, especially at night.

"They've filled in ditches too." Loughlin pointed them out.

"And probably got a minefield around the goddamn house," Hog grunted. "You figger they want to keep us out?"

Franz Stael and his mother returned to the apartment to find it empty. Anton had gone and not left a note. That was not like him. There was no sign of a struggle but the front door had been battered in. It looked as if someone had kicked it. In the living room a chair was overturned.

And in the bedroom a window was open. Franz said, "He went down the fire escape when they came to the door. He's safe."

"But where is he?"

"I don't know—but I do know we've got to get away from here as fast as we can."

"We can't go and leave him!"

"Be sensible, Mother. They'll kill both of us if they find us. Is there anything here you want?"

She gathered up a few things and he hurried her down to the van. His father had sent him to get the documents earlier, and he had luckily taken his mother, who had wanted to buy a few things on the way. His father was a resourceful man; he would know what to do. He would get out of Frankfurt, Franz was sure of it.

Karl Neff thought to return to the Stael apartment, but he had no wish to be grabbed by the police and interrogated. He had no answers to the questions they would ask. Someone had surely called the police after the noise he'd made kicking in the door.

Where were the documents? Maybe he should have searched the apartment instead of running after Anton Stael. No, he had done the right thing. Surely Stael would not keep such precious papers in the apartment. And now they belonged to Stael's son... who certainly must know what they are. Neff recalled very clearly the man with the submachine gun.

Neff had apparently dropped out of sight. None of Carol's snoops, spies and informers had turned up anything. He had not gone back to Odile Buchon's digs; he might have left the country altogether.

With von Schiller's organization after him, it might be the wisest course.

"We can assume it," Stone said, "but watch out for him just the same."

Their objective turned toward von Schiller since it was established that he was the kingpin.

# Chapter Twenty-five

Von Schiller was unhappy with the reports he was receiving. They were too sketchy, not detailed enough. These were the times he deeply regretted the death of Danzig. The little potato face had been thorough and efficient. Each job he had done had been carried out promptly and with deadly precision—and no clues left behind that could be traced to him.

He called on Carlo Vanner to shape things up.

The next target had been decided upon. He was Arnold Falen, the American ambassador to West Germany. He was to be taken and held for ransom.

Money had been secretly passed and the ambassador's schedule had been copied down. He was to deliver a speech in Barth, a town seventy miles from Bonn. He would go there by automobile; a spot had already been selected to grab him.

Carlo arrived in Bonn and tightened up the arrangements. The ambassador's car would be forced off the road and the prisoner would be taken to Osten, outside of Frankfurt.

Then a diversion would be made, a telephone call from Hamburg, in the other direction, asking for money, saying the ambassador was safe in Hamburg. . . .

Carlo could find no fault with the plan and it was put into operation.

* * *

Ambassador Falen and several aides worked over the speech he was to give in Barth, preparing it to Falen's satisfaction. It was largely political and he would take with him the minister of political affairs, John Fellowes, who was an affable sort. It was a seventy-mile ride to Barth. Falen would be much happier with Fellowes than with General Burrows, who was an old grouch most of the time.

But the afternoon before he was to go to Barth, Falen began to feel poorly and started vomiting. He was rushed to the infirmary and put to bed. The diagnosis was food poisoning.

From his bed, Falen turned the speech over to his DCM, Deputy Chief of Mission Homer Elland.

The press was not told of the change for security reasons, and Elland and Fellowes set out for Barth the next morning in a Mercedes from the motor pool, with a BMW containing two State Department security guards in front.

Thirty miles out of Bonn the road made a rather abrupt change, rounding a corner with a high stone wall on one side and a ramshackle barn on the other. As they came around the corner an old and battered Ford lurched into the road and the Mercedes's driver was forced to brake hard; the Mercedes rocked to a stop, its front bumper against the side of the old Ford.

Instantly four men surrounded the Mercedes and the driver was pulled out at gunpoint. A harsh voice told the two passengers to stay where they were.

The BMW had moved on a hundred yards or so, then the driver braked and turned the car. As he did so two men fired bursts from submachine guns. The windshield shattered and the car swerved and ran off the road into a ditch and stopped.

One of the four attackers slid behind the wheel of the Mercedes, two of the others got into the back, sitting on jump seats facing the Americans, and the fourth man got in the front beside the driver, who turned the car around and stepped on the gas.

Elland said, "Where the hell are you taking us?"

"Where you'll be safe," Carlo Vanner replied.

"Do you know who we are?"

"Certainly. You are the ambassador and—"

"I am not the ambassador. I am his assistant, the DCM."

Carlo stared at the man. He did not resemble the photos of the ambassador!

"You've got the wrong man," Elland said. "The ambassador is sick in bed. I'm taking his place."

Carlo sighed. He looked at the second man. "And who are you?"

"John Fellowes, minister of political affairs."

The driver spoke. "Do we continue?"

"Of course we continue," Vanner snapped. "Do as we planned."

"What do you want with us?" Elland demanded.

"Money," Vanner said.

The driver of the Mercedes had not been harmed. He had been yanked out of the car, then ignored. He was armed, but against four men with automatic weapons resistance would have been suicide.

He had flopped on the ground, and he stayed there till the Mercedes moved off. Then he got up and ran to the BMW. Both security guards were dead, riddled with bullets.

A truck and two cars stopped and the driver asked the occupants to telephone the police; he would stay with the car.

A motorcycle officer arrived in an hour, then two carloads of police and detectives. The American embassy in Bonn was radioed and news of the kidnapping was given out to the press.

The driver was able to give a very good description of two of the four; photos were shown him and he picked out Carlo Vanner. "This is one of them—probably the leader."

The police suspected that Vanner was a member of von Schiller's organization. But they did not find him when they raided the estate at Osten. None of von Schiller's men would admit they knew Vanner.

The Mercedes was found abandoned on a sidestreet in Barth. It had been carefully rubbed clean of fingerprints.

Later that day a letter arrived at the embassy demanding

eight hundred thousand dollars in ransom for the two men, Elland and Fellowes.

By a curious coincidence, a letter also arrived at von Schiller's big house with a copy of another very damaging document and a demand for money.

After reading it, von Schiller raged. Anton Stael was dead but his son carried on the vendetta.

"I will never be free of this man," von Schiller said, "until he is dead." He examined the letter. "There are no instructions. Is this all?"

"I expect the instructions will follow," Uto Schrenck replied. "If he wants cash we may have a chance to grab him." He lit a cigarette. "But we must also get our hands on all the documents. We do not know how many he has."

"The Reich was to last a thousand years," von Schiller growled. "Who would have thought then it was going to be but a dozen?" He paced the room. "Yes, every paper must be found and destroyed. Every member of that family must be destroyed." He paused. "Where is Carlo now?"

"We have him safe, General. We will change his appearance and give him new papers."

"Good. The two prisoners are at Osten?"

"Yes. They were taken there in a tradesman's truck long after dark and are held in one of the secret rooms."

"Very good."


Franz Stael worried that, being an amateur, he would make stupid errors. But the plan he evolved for receiving the money from von Schiller seemed to him to be foolproof.

Receiving the money was the critical thing. Von Schiller's men would kill him on sight, he was positive, and then go after his mother and the other documents. His plan should forestall that.

He picked the place very carefully, drew a practice map and wrote out instructions...and read them over a hundred times. He could see no way the general's men could get at him.

In the instructions he stated the money would be sent to him exactly in this manner and no other, on a certain day and time, or the German press—the international press—would be flooded with evidences of von Schiller's bloody past. He assured the reader of the letter he meant what he said.

He demanded that one million dollars be placed in a small trunk, and gave explicit instructions for its delivery.

# Chapter Twenty-six

The kidnapping of Elland and Fellowes was a shock to everyone, and several raids by the police were instituted immediately. But nothing turned up.

A ransom letter was received at the embassy, and the gist of it given to the media along with the curt reply that the United States government would not negotiate with kidnappers. No ransom would be paid. This policy, said the papers, had been initiated by Mr. Kissinger as secretary of state, and had been followed by the government ever since.

Stone, Hog Wiley and Loughlin went to visit the scene, then read the report of the driver. He had been sent back to the States at his own request; his report held nothing new.

It was obvious that the route to be taken by the two cars was known, even though it had been confidential. The embassy staff was investigating this avenue. The ambassador made a statement to the press that the kidnappers would be brought to justice; the German police concurred in this.

No mention of von Schiller was made in the press, not even speculation, but the big house was put under observation around the clock.

Anton Stael was dead but it was the opinion of many that his son would carry on his work. With this in mind, Stone, Loughlin and Hog set about tracing them—the son and his mother.

Working backward from the place Stael was killed, they canvassed the apartments till they found the one where he and the family had lived for a short time. They talked to all the neighbors and learned nothing. The Staels—under another name—had kept to themselves.

But they struck pay dirt in the form of a maintenance man named Jon Kodel, who lived alone in the basement apartment. Kodel had a list of names and, what was more important, a list of all automobile license numbers.

He had the number of the Staels' van.

Stone said, "We'll have to give the number to the police. They've got the people to make this kind of large-scale sweep. It would take us four million years to look at every van in Germany."

"I agree." Carol nodded. "I'll make the request first thing."

Every policeman was on the lookout for the Stael van. Every policeman in all of the Federal Republic was notified of the plate number, but the information was not given to the media for obvious reasons.

Franz Stael and his mother had driven to the village of Bruck and rented a suburban house. The house was on the edge of the marshes that extended for miles east and west and were five or six miles across. The marshes were navigable for the most part, and with the house came a rowboat that had been used by various tenants for fishing.

Franz rented a motorboat and with it towed the old rowboat two miles into the marshes and left it with a tall pole and an orange flag on it.

Von Schiller was to have the trunk with the money deposited on the boat. Franz would then go and pick up the money.

Von Schiller was warned to have his men stay at least a mile from the rowboat while Franz went for the money. The marshes were flat and it would be easy to see whether he did or not.

Franz was absolutely certain that von Schiller's men would have the rowboat surrounded a mile distant, so no one—in a power boat or not—would be able to escape his guns. Franz would be shot and his body weighted and dropped into the marshes and that would be the last heard of him.

That was what he faced. Franz had barely made his preparations when the day was at hand.

Von Schiller's man was to deposit the trunk with the money at noon.

And it went off like clockwork. Franz, with powerful binoculars, saw the boat approach the old rowboat, and a dark, bulky object was tipped into it. The boat then pulled away.

When Franz was satisfied that it was a mile distant, he nudged the helicopter pilot. "Now!"

The chopper zoomed in and hovered only a few feet above the rocking rowboat as the rotors beat the murky marsh water. Franz slid down a rope ladder, attached a net and rope to the trunk and climbed back into the helicopter. He pulled up the trunk as the pilot lifted the chopper.

They soared to five thousand feet and headed east.

As they climbed Franz was able to spot other boats. He had been right. Von Schiller had surrounded the spot. He grinned, thinking how they must be swearing. . . .

The pilot set the chopper down in Mainz and Franz paid him off. His mother had left that morning in the van and would meet him in the city later.

There was just one thing left to do. Franz Stael did not want this life. He did not want to live with constant fear as his father had. He did not want to continue risking his life, or his mother's, at the hands of such ruthless men as von Schiller. He would secure the remaining documents in a package, then mail them to the authorities. There would be no message attached. They would finally be free.

Then they would drive to Holland.

# Chapter Twenty-seven

The informer at Osten, Carol Jenner told them, was sure there was someone at the estate being held in secret.

"He says *someone*, but there could be two men, Elland and Fellowes."

Stone said, "But didn't the police search the place already?"

"Yes, but these old houses have secret rooms. It would take an expert to find them."

"How many of von Schiller's men are there?"

"The informant says eleven, including Dicot, the leader, and a house cleaner and a cook."

"Only three to one," Loughlin observed. "Not bad odds."

"So the police have been there—and probably won't go back without concrete evidence," Stone said.

Carol agreed. "That's right. If we could prove Elland and Fellowes *are* being held there, the cops will go in and get them. No matter what it takes."

"That leaves it up to us," Loughlin said, shrugging. "When do we go?"

"Tonight. Let's get started. It's a long drive."

They had been to Osten before but expected changes. They left the van several miles away in a wood and hiked along the road in the dark, on the lookout for a patrol.

It came, as they knew it would—a small Japanese car

with two men inside, and a searchlight that clicked on and off whenever the man beside the driver took a fancy.

They lay prone in a weedy field as it went past, then crossed the field toward the house, which was well lighted. The outer buildings, however, were dark, and it was no trick to crawl up to them.

Stone put his head around the side of the shed they lay against. It was fifty yards to the house but there was plenty of shrubbery in between. It looked like a garden. There was even a kind of gazebo off to the left.

Where the hell would they put the two prisoners?

He studied the house; most of the windows were dark. Two on the lower floor showed dim lights as well as one in the back, near a door. He could see no walking guards. Maybe there were none.

Hog slithered up beside him and tugged his elbow. "Two cars a-sittin' over there under them trees." Hog pointed. "Might be a good idea to unplug 'em."

"Right."

"Which way you headin'?"

"For the back door."

"See you there." Hog slipped away.

Stone motioned to Loughlin and moved toward the rear of the house.

There were yard lights here and there, but not like the last time they'd been here. They were able to gain the side of the house in shadow and they moved toward the rear door. Loughlin investigated each window they came to but all were securely latched.

There was a wide porch around the rear door and a single naked bulb illuminating it. Peering around carefully, Stone stepped onto the porch and unscrewed the bulb. The porch went dark.

Loughlin tried the door. It was locked but he drew his knife and chewed into the wood. He had it open in a moment.

They slipped inside. There was an inner door, but it too was quickly opened. They were in a large kitchen that smelled strongly of cooked food.

They were equipped with silenced pistols. Stone poked

his into a hallway that was dimly lighted. Maybe most of the house's inhabitants were in bed. He could hear music coming from somewhere, probably a radio or TV set.

The hall was short, with a door on either side, both closed. The hall ended in a large, almost circular room with two archways. He remembered nothing of this; maybe last time they'd been on the other side of the large house. Loughlin pointed to a staircase, and Stone debated for a moment. Should they go upstairs? Maybe it would be better to investigate this floor first.

He said softly, "Where would you build a secret room?"

"In London."

Stone looked at him and Loughlin shook his head.

Leaning against the wall, Stone sighed. It would take a month to measure every wall in this house and compare notes—*without* an enemy around every corner. Their best bet would probably be to capture someone and make him talk.

But that was out of the question tonight.

He moved through one of the arches and found himself in a huge sitting room. There was a blazing fireplace at the far side and no other light. The music was coming from somewhere close to the fire, and Stone stopped short, seeing a man's head outlined on a big easy chair. The man was looking into the fire.

But some sixth sense apparently alerted the man. He sat up and looked around before they could duck. It was von Schiller!

In the next second he fired a report and a moment later a bell clanged. Stone said, "Shit!" He followed Loughlin into another room that was full of trophies and glass cases. Now the entire place was alerted. They would play hell getting out!

They turned into a wide carpeted hall with tall plants. At the far end was what looked to be a door, and Stone turned toward it.

Loughlin yelled and Stone hit the floor as automatic fire slashed the air over their heads. He rolled, firing as he did so. There were shouts from the other direction. He rolled against the door, opened it and slithered inside. Loughlin was on the far side of the hall in a doorway, reloading.

"Saw three of 'em," he said in a conversational tone. "Think we hit one."

Stone was in a music room; it was empty except for a piano and some electronic equipment. It was an interior room; there were no windows. He looked into the hall and could see no one.

Loughlin said, "There might be a way out of here . . ."

Stone nodded and ran across the hall, drawing a late shot that was wild. As he gained the room on Loughlin's side there were shots from outside the house.

"Hog's getting their attention," the Brit said, grinning. "Now they don't know how many of us there are."

"But they know where we are."

"Righto. Well, let's go this way . . ." Loughlin crossed the room and stepped into a very narrow, dark hall that ran toward the back of the house. He ran toward the end and Stone followed, glancing back. As he neared the end of the hall, he saw a shadow detach itself from the wall. He pushed Loughlin around the corner and tumbled after him as a long burst of fire smashed the wall at their elbows.

"Bloody close!" Loughlin said, sucking in his breath.

Stone slid his pistol around the corner and squeezed off five shots. The shadow had disappeared. He reloaded quickly, watching the hall.

Beside him, Loughlin said, "Here now, what's this?"

"What's what?"

Loughlin had his eye to the holes made in the wall by the automatic fire. "There's a room in there!"

Stone looked. It was true—a tiny room with a dim light. But there was no door. It was a wood-paneled room; probably the door was concealed.

"Bingo!" he muttered.

Stone pulled back a combat boot and sent a powerful kick that knocked a hole in the plaster and bent in some of the wood.

"Here, let me lend a hand," Loughlin grunted. "I mean, a foot."

The two of them had a hole kicked in the wall seconds

later. Loughlin ducked inside while Stone covered their backs.

"They're in here," Loughlin called out.

Stone ducked in after the Brit, who already had one of the hostages, John Fellowes, hoisted over his shoulder in a fireman's carry. Stone heaved the second man, Elland, over his back similarly. He and Loughlin slipped back out into the hallway.

Fellowes and Elland were drugged unconscious, as expected; von Schiller's people would find them easier to handle that way. Stone didn't mind having them that way either; less chance of the two hostages buying a round during their own rescue.

Stone and Loughlin got the pair outside. The house and environs were coming to life, men running, shouting in the night, lights going on.

They started away from the house.

Sudden firing from their left caused a ricochet to go screaming into the night. Stone pointed and they hurried toward the sound. It came again, long bursts of automatic fire that ripped into a small outbuilding.

Then Hog Wiley moved from behind a tree and fired several shots, and the automatic fire stopped abruptly.

Stone gave a whistle and the big man turned and dropped to one knee. In a second he answered. They met him in the clump of trees. Hog was grinning. "Been keepin' these here jaspers off your, uh, backs." He saw the two unconscious men clearly then for the first time and his hairy face split wide in a grin. "Looks like you did all right, bros. Time to git."

They pulled back to where Hog had parked the van.

Floodlights were going on around the house, but by that time the team and the rescued hostages were moving out without headlights, and no one saw them go; Hog had stashed the wheels well over a dip in the terrain, shielded from view of the grounds.

They went a ways before Hog switched on the lights.

"Pull off the road here, Hog," Stone instructed.

"You got it." Wiley did as he was told.

Loughlin frowned. "What's the play?"

"I want von Schiller," said Stone. "He's the key to this. We nail that Nazi scum and the killing will stop because the money supply will dry up and the brains will be out of the picture one way or another."

"He's overdue for somethin' or other," Hog snorted.

"So what do we do with our sleeping beauties?" Loughlin asked with a nod toward Fellowes and Elland. They had not moved since they were placed side by side in the rear of the van.

"We set them right here," Stone said with a nod at the cluster of trees well off the highway. "Radio Carol to set the play in action. I want the police coming down on that place hard. Tell them where to find these two."

"What about us?" Loughlin asked.

"And what about the Kraut?" Hog asked.

"We wait right here," Stone told Loughlin. He told Hog, "Von Schiller will be hightailing it out of there, and past here, any second. Let's see where he takes us."

They hurriedly unloaded the two out-cold ex-hostages, and just in time.

Three cars came screeching out of the grounds behind them and went sailing past.

# Chapter Twenty-eight

They followed the three cars into the countryside; on the Autobahn the limo was like an arrow, moving at speeds over one hundred miles an hour. The other two vehicles could not keep up.

It took an hour to cross the border and the limo was in sight again. It headed southwest, with the two smaller cars tagging along behind.

"They know we're here," Loughlin said, using the binocs. "One of them's watching us with a glass."

Hog growled, "Watch for an ambush." He checked the magazine on his Uzi.

Hog was a prophet. They came around a bend and the two cars were straddling the road, deep ditches on either side. The limo must have continued on. As they came into view, automatic fire greeted them.

Stone swore, halting the car and backing instantly. Bullets smashed the radiator before he had gone ten feet. Hog dived out of the car on one side, Loughlin the other. Stone swerved the car and dived out to follow Hog. The car was riddled and in a moment it went up in an orange flash as the petrol tank exploded.

They were safe from hot lead in the ditch. It was weedy but not wet.

Hog scuttled toward the two blocking cars. Stone halted to peer at the enemy through a screen of scrub. He counted six men. Three were conferring beyond the cars; the others were lying across hoods and trunks, rifles ready.

He saw Hog rise up and fire. Two of the men by the cars disappeared, one flinging his rifle into the air. The third man fired at Hog, slicing weeds above his head as Hog grinned at Stone.

Then Loughlin fired from the far side of the road and one of the men behind the cars fell. Loughlin concentrated his fire on one of the cars, smashing glass and the engine. Hog rose and fired with him and two of the men turned and ran down the road, abandoning the cars.

Four men were dead and one car was a wreck. The other was untouched. It was the old Mercedes they had followed in days past. They piled the weapons in the back of the Mercedes, pulled the bodies off the road and left the wrecked car as it was.

"What about them two?" Hog asked, pointing along the road.

"We don't have time to chase them," Stone replied. "Let 'em go." He got behind the wheel and started the engine.

"Where's von Schiller going?" Loughlin asked. "He must have a destination."

"He's gonna hole up somewheres," Hog said, "hopin' this'll all blow over."

Stone drove as fast as he dared but they were probably half an hour behind the limo now. But there were few limos in this part of Germany; it might not be difficult to trace.

They asked in each town or village and received the same answers: *Ja,* the black limo had passed through. . . .

Until at one village the answers were: No. No limo had come along the road.

Von Schiller had turned off.

The authorities had received Franz's package and had verified the authenticity of the papers. And in no time at all the press was informed and headlines proclaimed von Schiller's criminal record. The deaths of thousands were attributed to him.

But he could not be found. The press speculated that he had long since left the country and persons came forward to say they had seen him at such and such an airport. . . .

Forty-year-old pictures of him were published; foreign nations were notified. People loyal to von Schiller, such as those at Osten—where the two diplomats, Elland and Fellowes, had been found—were rounded up and put into jail.

But where was von Schiller?

Von Schiller was in a country house that had belonged to one of his wartime associates, Lieutenant Colonel Notzing. Notzing was dead but his widow had been every bit as avid a Nazi as her husband. She was proud to conceal von Schiller.

"They will not find you here, General. But even if they do stumble on this house, there is a light plane that will carry you to Austria—or anywhere else in Europe."

"You are too kind, my dear." Schiller kissed her hand. He was delighted to know about the plane. It was always good to have an ace in the hole. Carlo Vanner had been one of the six men in the two following cars. He had gotten away under fire, he said on the telephone, but four men were dead. He thought they had been followed by the three Americans. Carlo would come to the Notzing house as quickly as he could.

But it was distressing news all the same. Those damned three Americans! No one seemed able to kill them!

The Notzing house was situated on a hill overlooking the countryside, with blue mountains all around, a beautiful site. But it had not been designed as a fort. The surrounding woods came almost to the doors and the outside lights were few. The road to the house was a very narrow one-way track that branched off from the main road in a tangle of trees. It was not marked.

There were many such roads and many of them led nowhere, he was informed. But probably he should not stay here long. . . .

# Chapter Twenty-nine

There was no way of knowing whether von Schiller had turned off to take another road, or whether his destination was near. Stone and his men spent the rest of the afternoon pursuing fruitless tracks. There were a dozen turnoffs and each one had to be investigated.

But they came at last to a tangle of trees where a dusty road darted into a wood, and Hog, jogging ahead, found fresh tire marks.

"This ain't a connecting road," he said. "This here goes to a house. Bet your ass."

Stone backed the van into the trees and they went ahead on foot. The road led in a circling path uphill for a mile or so, then Hog, in the lead, halted, arms outstretched. When they came up to him, he pointed. "There's the house."

They could see part of a chimney where smoke was slowly rising, drifting up to blend with the hazy sky.

"All right," Stone said, "let's nose around, get the lay of it and meet back here at the road."

"Wilco." Loughlin nodded. "I'll go with you, Texas."

"Stay the hell out of trouble," Stone warned. He turned to his right into the trees. It was a thick pine wood with birds chattering overhead. In five minutes he approached the house and squatted to examine it. It was a well-built three-story house with deep set windows, dormers and four chimneys. The area around the house was bricked, with plants in large pots here and there. It looked very comfortable in an affluent way. There was no one in sight.

He faded back and moved to his right, toward the rear of the house. Was von Schiller here?

There was a half-covered pool behind the house, with colorful umbrellas and a dozen poolside chairs. Two men were talking near the pool; they looked like guards. As he watched them they separated, each going around the house in a different direction.

Stone shook his head. Piss-poor security.

There was a chain-link fence between him and the grounds but it could be vaulted in a moment. It had probably been put up to keep wildlife out.

He circled the rear of the extensive house, meeting Hog and Loughlin near the long garages. In the brick courtyard in front of the garages was the black limo they had followed. A man in shirtsleeves was polishing it.

"He's here," Hog said. "How do we get him out?"

Stone mused, "There can't be many guns in there. . . . Of course, the big brass wants him alive. That'll make it harder. Let's get up close tonight and see if we can find a soft spot."

They went back to view the pool area, finding a comfortable glade where they could see without being seen. A man was sitting at one of the tables reading a newspaper. Stone focused the binocs on him, a much younger man, dressed in a dark blue suit. He sipped a cup of coffee as he read.

When the man looked around suddenly, Stone lifted the glasses. The rear door of the house had opened and three men came out.

One of them was von Schiller.

He passed the glasses to the others for a look. Von Schiller and the others were enjoying a joke, apparently. They all sat around the table with the first man and one of them spread out papers. Von Schiller picked them up to read, then pulled out a pair of reading glasses and put them on.

They were probably two hundred yards from the table and slightly above it. The estate did not take up the entire crest of the hill but had been built with the view in mind.

Stone took the binoculars back and focused on von Schiller again.

He saw the man jerk in astonishment and heard the crack of a high-powered rifle at the same time.

Stone could not tell where the bullet had hit. One of the men at the table threw himself across von Schiller instantly, bearing him to the deck, as a second rifle shot slammed into the metal table.

Stone said, "See if you can find him!"

Hog and Loughlin took off instantly; Stone kept the binocs on the group by the pool. The sniper had been in the woods behind and probably above them. It had been a long shot, shooting downhill, probably the shooter was not an expert.

The men by the pool had pulled the table over and, using it as a blind, rushed von Schiller into the house.

There was no third shot.

Stone bit his lip, staring at the house. Could it have been Karl Neff? He thought it very likely. Neff might have known of this house—after all, he'd been with von Schiller for a long time, and he might have been here before and deduced that von Schiller might use it as a hideaway. It fit.

As the minutes ticked away he wondered if the men inside the house were planning a sortie to find the sniper. No one came out. Very odd.

Maybe von Schiller had been hit. But he didn't think so. The man's actions had not seemed like it. But from what he knew of the Nazi general it wasn't like him to lie down and let someone shoot at him.

Stone moved around the hill to keep the garages in sight. Maybe reinforcements were on the way.

Hog Wiley separated from Loughlin and hurried through the woods toward the place where he'd heard the sounds of the rifle. Did the sniper, whoever he was, know they were there? He doubted it. But maybe he did and thought he could shoot and get away. That meant he had transportation nearby.

Hog moved to his right, to get between the sniper and

the road. Loughlin had circled far to the left.

Hog came onto the road before he realized it, and loped along it, cocking the Uzi. He had been right. There was a car sitting in the road, facing downhill, about three hundred yards farther on.

And a moment later Neff burst from the trees and ran toward it. He was carrying a rifle.

Hog yelled and Neff jerked his head around, startled. Hog saw a white blur of face, then Neff halted and the rifle came up. Neff got off two quick shots before the Uzi stuttered. Neff's shots went wild but the burst from the Uzi cut him almost in half.

Hog walked toward the body and several minutes later Loughlin appeared. "What happened?"

Hog pointed, "He couldn't shoot his ass."

They dragged the body off the road and went back through the trees to the house.

Chewing his lower lip, Stone heard the distant shots . . . and the silence.

In the house, they heard the sounds too. Someone came to the rear door and looked out briefly. Then a man ran from the house to the garages and backed out a small BMW. In a moment von Schiller and two others came out and got into the car. It started down the hill and Stone hurried through the trees after it.

The BMW did not take the road to the highway; instead it turned right, running along a weed-grown two-track road that threaded its way through the trees. It was a bad road, with hard turns and ruts. Stone was easily able to keep up.

But the car did not go far.

It halted at a large, low barnlike building. Stone watched the men jump out of the car, swing open the doors of the brown building and go inside to wheel out a small airplane.

Von Schiller was about to make his getaway!

One of the men crawled inside the plane, and as Stone made his way down to the field, they started the engine. It roared into life and two men dragged the tail around, pointing the plane down the long airstrip.

Stone was still four or five hundred yards away when von Schiller got into the plane with the pilot. The others stood back as the plane taxied down the strip, running with the wind.

Stone swore, gritting his teeth. The plane was so close . . . and yet so far!

Then it stopped and turned, heading into the wind. The pilot revved the engine, then the plane began to move toward him. Stone ran onto the field, lifting the Uzi submachine gun. Out of the corner of his eye he saw the men by the hangar run to the BMW, but he paid them no attention.

Aiming at the engine, Stone fired a long shattering burst.

For a moment nothing seemed to happen. Then the plane bucked in the air. One wing came up and it turned slowly, and Stone could see long tongues of flame as the plane hurled itself to the ground, crashing in a huge orange blossom that turned into dense black smoke.

The sound of the crash was like an explosion—then a loud crackling as the flames ate everything greedily.

Stone stood there and watched, blowing out his breath.

*Goodbye, von Schiller. You son of a bitch.*

He turned to trudge back and join the others, letting the weariness begin to wash over him at the end of what had proved to be one hell of an endurance marathon. But, yeah, it *was* over.

The hostage takers were smashed.

The whole tangled web had been woven from new blood like Neff and sponsored by old-time rats like von Schiller, to cause blood baths using political rhetoric as a smoke screen for the real motive of generating more income for the human garbage who grew richer while the victims of terrorism died.

And Stone's team had recovered three M.I.A.'s. Eva Ullman, John Fellowes and Homer Elland.

The mission had served to make Stone even more aware of the shifting role of his team. They were still an off-the-record hard-punch combat unit specializing in covert search and rescue, but that area of operations was widening with every mission, it seemed.

Stone continued to keep an ear to the ground regarding his first commitment, M.I.A.'s in Southeast Asia, but no hard intel had come in lately to send him, Hog and Loughlin back there.

Stone knew that day would come.

In the meantime, he and his buddies would be where the hellfire was hottest.

That was the single certainty in Mark Stone's life.

The fight would continue.